VICTORIAN
MANSION
FLOWER SHOP™
MYSTERIES

Planted Evidence

Kristi Holl

AnniesFiction.com

Books in the Victorian Mansion Flower Shop Mysteries series

Library of Congress-in-Publication Data
Planted Evidence / by Kristi Holl
p. cm.
I. Title
                    2017964148

AnniesFiction.com
(800) 282-6643
Victorian Mansion Flower Shop Mysteries™
Series Creators: Shari Lohner, Janice Tate
Editor: Lorie Jones
Cover Illustrator: Bob Kayganich

10 11 12 13 14 | Printed in South Korea | 9 8 7 6 5 4

1

The Flower Patch glowed in the October sunlight, and Kaylee Bleu smiled in appreciation as she scanned the front of her flower shop, a repurposed Victorian mansion that was always stunning. Temperatures wouldn't drop to freezing for another few weeks, so the flowers on her wraparound porch still thrived. As she gazed down Main Street, she noticed more flowers blooming in profusion—in boxes, in wooden tubs along the curbs, and in baskets hanging from the light posts.

Kaylee had purchased the flower shop—along with her home, Wildflower Cottage—from her grandmother, and every day she felt grateful for her life on Orcas Island.

Bear, her adorable dachshund, licked her hand.

She rubbed his silky ears and straightened his orange-and-yellow striped bow tie before climbing the steps to the porch and unlocking the front door.

Inside The Flower Patch, Kaylee fluffed the pillows in the seating area where she held consultations and rearranged displays of handcrafted lavender goat milk soaps and rosewater body lotion. Then she cleaned the glass fronts of the refrigerated coolers where she stored cut flowers and finished arrangements.

Bear nudged her leg and gave a single bark. It was his signal that he was ready for his treat from the stash she kept in her office filing cabinet.

Kaylee smiled as she headed upstairs. "Good thing I have you to keep me grounded in what's important."

Bear trotted up the stairs behind her.

In her office, she checked her messages and e-mails, but she didn't have any that demanded immediate attention. It was a blessing to ease into her workday before customers' demands took over. However, Bear's dog biscuit needs were constant. The reddish-brown dachshund repeatedly nudged the file cabinet drawer with his nose.

"Don't hurt yourself. Here." Kaylee gave him a biscuit.

Bear carried it to his doggy bed in the corner. Curling up, he settled in to enjoy his treat.

Downstairs, Kaylee grabbed a broom and flipped the sign on the front door from *Closed* to *Open*. She gathered her dark-brown hair into a ponytail, then went outside and began sweeping the wide veranda that curved around two sides of The Flower Patch. Located on a corner on Main Street, her shop faced The Chandlery Gift Shop, a boutique that sold cards, stationery, candles, and postcards. Other shops, filled with local artisan crafts and a variety of specialized products, lined the quaint streets of Turtle Cove, Washington.

Kaylee leaned on her broom and gazed down the quiet street. Tourist crowds had thinned ever since children had returned to school. She picked a few wrinkled blossoms from her pots and hanging baskets of red *Impatiens walleriana*, then continued sweeping. Moving around to the side porch, she grabbed her watering can.

Without warning, a sheriff's car sped past her shop and pulled up outside The Velvet Box jewelry store. Sheriff Eddie Maddox and Deputy Nick Durham exited the car and strode inside.

What was going on over there that required the police? Was there a robbery in progress? Had they arrived without sirens so that a criminal wouldn't panic and shoot someone? Kaylee's friend Amanda Denman, who'd recently moved to town with her fifteen-year-old daughter, Madison, worked there. Had Amanda or anyone else already been hurt?

Kaylee dropped her watering can and whispered a prayer as she sprinted toward the store.

Two shoppers on the sidewalk stopped and stared as Kaylee raced by.

Heart pounding, she peered through the plate glass window that covered most of the jewelry store's otherwise-brick front. She noticed that the law officers had not drawn their guns, and she didn't see anyone who appeared to be a criminal. Sheriff Maddox was speaking to the store's owner, Joseph Liddon. Amanda stood at her employer's elbow.

Kaylee's gaze was riveted on Amanda's horrified expression. Were they bringing her bad news? Had Amanda's daughter been injured at school?

Kaylee pushed through the cluster of gawkers gathered on the sidewalk and burst inside. "Amanda, is everything all right? Is it Madison?" She hurried to her friend's side and slid an arm around her.

Amanda trembled, and her eyes had a wild look.

"Kaylee, could you wait outside?" Sheriff Maddox asked. Although in the past the sheriff had accepted Kaylee's help in her field of forensic botany, he obviously didn't find her presence necessary at the moment. "Mrs. Denman is fine."

"She's obviously *not* fine." Kaylee spoke evenly, trying to match his calm tone of voice. "What happened?"

Amanda's mouth trembled. "They think—"

"Please," Joseph Liddon interrupted. "This does not concern you."

Kaylee studied the store owner. His frosty smile chilled her. She'd never noticed before, but his protruding eyes reminded her of an aging frog, and the green shirt he wore today only made the resemblance more pronounced. She almost expected his tongue to dart out and catch a fly.

"They've accused me of theft," Amanda blurted out, flushed and breathless.

"What? That's ridiculous!" Kaylee zeroed in on Deputy Nick Durham, a friend of hers. "You can't be serious. Amanda would never steal anything."

Nick scratched his trimmed goatee and darted a glance at his boss.

The sheriff's expression was impossible to read. He cleared his throat, the deep rumble a clear order for his deputy not to say a word. "Step aside." He motioned Kaylee to stand by the front door. "If you interrupt again, you'll need to leave."

Amanda gave Kaylee such a pleading look that Kaylee bit back her protest. Fuming, she moved near the door.

A young couple by a display of engagement rings gaped at the proceedings, as if they were witnessing a reality TV show. The woman whipped out her phone to take pictures or a video, and Kaylee scowled at her. She quickly put the phone away.

"Now, Mrs. Denman," the sheriff said, "pick up where you left off before we were interrupted."

Amanda glanced at Kaylee, gulped, and turned back to the sheriff. "I helped close the store last night, the same as always."

"Not *exactly* the same," Joseph cut in.

Sheriff Maddox skewered him with a black look. "You'll get your chance in a minute."

Joseph's bulging eyes seemed to protrude even more, and he rocked on the balls of his feet. But he fell silent.

Amanda took a deep breath. "As far as I remember, I closed the store with Mr. Liddon the same as always. He locked the front door at six, we both covered the less expensive jewelry with flannel cloths, and we carried the most expensive pieces to the safe to lock up for the night."

"And the safe is located where?" The sheriff shook his pen and then wrote in his small spiral notebook.

"In Mr. Liddon's office."

Maddox glanced up from his notebook. "Were you ever alone in the office?"

"I don't believe so." She turned to Joseph. "Was I?"

"No she wasn't," he admitted.

"Then what was different about last night?" Nick asked.

"I'll tell you what was different," Joseph said. "I was in the office the whole time, but while Mrs. Denman finished placing necklaces in the safe, I sat at my desk to finish some bookwork. The safe is located directly behind my desk, so I didn't actually *see* her put the remaining jewelry in there." He shot her an accusing look. "That must have been when she, uh, pocketed the necklaces. It would have been an easy thing to do."

"But I didn't!" The desperate note in Amanda's voice made Kaylee wince.

Sheriff Maddox glanced from Amanda to Joseph. "Who locked the safe last night then?"

"Mr. Liddon always does," Amanda said. "But last night—for the first time—he continued working on the ledgers and told me to give the dial a twirl when I was done. So I did."

"Or did you barely close the safe door so you could open it again later?" Joseph retorted.

Kaylee clenched her fists, wishing she could box Joseph's ears.

"No, I twirled the dial," Amanda insisted. "Then I got my coat and left by the back door because I'd parked in the alley."

The sheriff nodded at the store owner. "What about when you opened the safe this morning?"

Joseph frowned. "The safe *was* locked when I came to work." Then he brightened. "She must have slipped the jewelry into her pocket *before* locking the safe. I was concentrating on the books and didn't notice. Now I know why she left the instant she closed the safe."

"I always leave right away," Amanda stated. "And last night

my daughter was waiting on me at the ferry after a trip for school, so I had to hurry over to pick her up."

Sheriff Maddox ran a hand through his black hair, which was peppered with gray. "Mr. Liddon, are you positive the missing pieces of jewelry were here last night when you locked up?"

"I'm positive. I'd taken out two whole trays of our most expensive items to display for Mrs. Margaret Fox. She tried on half a dozen pieces before buying a matching ruby ring and necklace. When she left at six, the other pieces were still on top of the glass case." Joseph puffed out his chest. "And before you ask, no other customers were in the store after Mrs. Fox left."

"I see." The sheriff jotted down another note. "Do you agree with your employer's account of the customers, Mrs. Denman?"

Amanda nodded. She seemed to be almost in a daze.

Kaylee cringed at Amanda's silent admission. Maybe she read too many mysteries, but she wished Amanda had refrained from answering questions and asked for a lawyer instead. Kaylee was troubled at how her friend had seemed to shrink a bit with each question, as if she were already defeated.

The sheriff slipped his notebook into his pocket. "It appears that you had both the means and the opportunity to steal the jewelry."

Kaylee dug her fingernails into her palms. Means and opportunity? She couldn't argue with that, but surely something was missing. Sheriff Maddox hadn't mentioned a motive.

Her heart sank. If the authorities dug into Amanda's bank accounts, they'd soon discover that her debt load provided her with ample motive.

Kaylee couldn't stand it anymore. "This is all circumstantial. You have no proof at all."

Joseph jabbed a finger at her. "Since you're the one who recommended that I hire her, your opinion is worth exactly nothing."

The sheriff silenced them both with an icy stare. "I was

getting to the need for proof before filing any charges. I'll obtain a search warrant for Mrs. Denman's home." He faced Amanda. "I want you to stay here in the store until we have a chance to search your house."

"I don't have the missing jewelry." Amanda was near tears. "I have nothing to hide. You don't need a warrant. I'll let you in right now, and you can search all you like. You won't find anything."

Alarms went off in Kaylee's head. That sounded dangerous. She had no doubt that Amanda was telling the truth, but shouldn't she have a lawyer present for her own protection?

When Amanda was led to the sheriff's car, Kaylee touched her arm. "I'll be right behind you." She ran back to the flower shop, grabbed her purse and locked the shop, then sped across town to Amanda's rented cottage.

The sheriff and deputy were already out of their car.

"You stay in the car," Sheriff Maddox instructed Amanda.

Kaylee followed them to the back door, where Nick stopped her. "You can't come in, but you can wait in the patrol car with your friend if you want."

Kaylee gestured to the back door. "Look. Her lock's broken."

"So it is. But there's no telling when that happened."

Kaylee leaned closer. Was it possible that the sheriff had just done it? But no, why would he? Amanda would have given him her house keys. Kaylee joined Amanda in the back seat of the squad car. Squeezing Amanda's hand, Kaylee sat beside her in silence and waited.

They didn't have to wait long.

Sheriff Maddox stepped outside the back door, something sparkly dangling from his hand.

"Oh no," Amanda whispered.

The sheriff motioned for them both to get out of the car. "We found this emerald necklace in your tea canister."

"That's impossible." Amanda bit down on her quivering lower lip.

"Of course it is." Kaylee put her hands on her hips. "Surely you can see it was planted on Amanda. Otherwise she never would have invited you to search her house without a warrant."

Sheriff Maddox slipped the jewelry into an evidence bag. "Unless her cooperation was designed to make her appear innocent."

Kaylee fought to keep her expression respectful when she wanted to roll her eyes instead. "If Amanda had stolen it, do you really think she couldn't have found a better hiding place than a tea canister?" She pointed at the back entry. "Did Nick show you the door? The lock's broken. It's obvious to me that someone broke in and planted the necklace where you couldn't possibly miss it."

"Or she broke the lock herself to make it look like there had been an intruder," Sheriff Maddox replied. "Either way, it's secured now."

Kaylee bit her tongue. It wouldn't do any good to get into an argument with the sheriff. It would most likely make things even worse for Amanda. She waited helplessly while Amanda got into the back of the sheriff's car. She sat, hunched over, as if trying to make herself too small to be noticed.

After watching them disappear down the street, Kaylee noticed the pain in her chest and realized she'd been holding her breath. She inhaled some deep breaths, then climbed into her SUV and headed back to The Flower Patch.

Three days later, Kaylee was still stunned at what had happened to Amanda. Although the morning was clear and crisp, menacing clouds lurked on the horizon of her mind. While fall color on Orcas Island would peak soon, her personal world felt gray. Sighing, Kaylee trudged up the front steps to The Flower Patch, stooped to retrieve *The Orcas Gazette* on the porch, and unlocked the door.

Bear, dressed in a black bow tie featuring tiny pumpkins, nearly tripped her by wrapping his leash around her ankles and dashing inside.

She dropped his leash as the headline on the front page leaped out at her: *Local Woman Arrested in Jewelry Theft*. The story filled three columns, and under the headline was Amanda's photo, her brow furrowed over frightened eyes. Kaylee barely recognized her friend's face.

She read the article. Although the newspaper got the facts straight, Kaylee knew that the implication was 100 percent wrong.

The sheriff's department arrested Amanda Denman at her home in Turtle Cove for the theft of several necklaces and rings from The Velvet Box jewelry store, where she has been employed as a clerk for one month. Although Mrs. Denman denied taking the jewelry, a search of her home turned up the missing emerald necklace. Two diamond necklaces and three diamond rings, with a combined estimated value of $18,000, are still missing. The Velvet Box owner, Joseph Liddon, has offered a substantial reward for the return of all the jewelry.

Inside the shop, she pocketed her keys and tossed the weekly newspaper on the counter, feeling sick over this happening to her friend. She shook her head as she hung up her down-filled jacket and flipped on the lights on the first floor. Although it dispelled the interior shadows of the shop, it didn't shift the gloom that settled over her like a wool blanket. Mentally giving herself a good shake, she unclipped Bear's leash and hung it on a hook. "Come on," she said to him. "I can't fix Amanda's situation today, but I can tackle our work and get you a treat."

Bear's ears perked up at his favorite word, and he barked enthusiastic agreement.

If only I could solve Amanda's problem so easily.

Later Bear followed Kaylee out to the wraparound porch. Using the cloth tucked into her back pocket, she dusted the white wooden rockers and wicker tables grouped on the porch. After that, she watered the pots of red *Impatiens walleriana* (or "busy Lizzies" as Grandma always called them). She was so used to her routine that she didn't have to think, and as she moved from planter to planter, her gaze was continually drawn to the jewelry store across the street. Kaylee studied the scene of the crime, wishing she could come up with a plan to exonerate her friend.

Would she ever be able to look at The Velvet Box again without picturing Amanda being led to the police car parked out front in full view of every customer in the store and pedestrian on the sidewalk?

Now she regretted convincing Amanda to move to Turtle Cove. According to Amanda, Kaylee had sounded like Turtle Cove's Chamber of Commerce as she'd gushed about Orcas Island's stunning ocean shorelines, emerald-green forests, sparkling lakes, spectacular wildlife, and scenic vineyards. Kaylee admitted she was biased. She'd been in love with the island since she was a child visiting her grandparents.

Over Labor Day weekend, Amanda had arrived with her daughter, Madison. Amanda's determined smile hadn't quite touched her eyes. Her husband of twenty years had left her high and dry, his heavy debts wiping both of them out financially. Kaylee had urged her to come to Turtle Cove to make a fresh start and recuperate, hoping the soothing salty breezes and the warmth of the small town's residents would work its healing magic on Amanda's heart.

Kaylee's plan had gone swimmingly at first, and she'd even helped her friend get a sales job at The Velvet Box. Amanda had enjoyed helping customers buy engagement rings and anniversary gifts, and over the past weeks, the island environment had put color in her cheeks and a tiny spring in her step.

Until the robbery.

Although the newspaper article said that the police investigation was continuing, Kaylee had her doubts. If they were still investigating, why had they arrested Amanda already? She thought Sheriff Maddox seemed prematurely satisfied that he'd found the right person.

"Hi, Kaylee! Beautiful morning, isn't it?"

Kaylee whirled around as she was jerked out of her anxious thoughts. Heart pounding like a jackhammer, she picked up the broom and watering can. She smiled and waved at the widowed sisters across the street who were opening up The Chandlery Gift Shop.

Penelope Cole and Sylvia Rosenthal were both in their sixties and still had a trace of a Georgian accent, but that was where their similarities ended. Penelope's full figure was a testament to her love of pie baking, and her sweet disposition attracted people of all ages. She often brought her calico cat, Peaches, with her to the store. Her younger sister, Sylvia, was on the slender side and wore her white hair in a short bob, and she was just as organized as Penelope was flaky. Sylvia was not fond of cats, but she tolerated her sister's.

The sisters had taken Amanda and Madison under their wings, even letting Madison stay with them while Amanda was in jail. Kaylee suspected that Penelope would have gladly adopted them both.

Back inside The Flower Patch, Bear climbed the stairs, and Kaylee guessed he was ready for a nap. She put the broom away, slamming the closet door twice before it would stay closed. All the doors were swollen after the unusually large amount of rain they'd received so far this month.

Out front, the bell over the shop door chimed.

Kaylee glanced at her watch. Amanda, out on bail, had planned to drop in this morning. Kaylee snatched the morning newspaper from where she'd left it on the counter and buried it in the bottom of the wastebasket.

She wished she could make her friend's troubles disappear that quickly.

2

Kaylee pasted on a cheery smile and hurried to the front door. "Oh!" She stopped abruptly. "It's you."

"Not sure how I should take that." Reese Holt grinned, making his blue eyes crinkle at the corners. "You were obviously expecting someone else."

Despite the chilly weather, Reese was dressed in worn jeans and a T-shirt, with a flannel shirt open over it. He was a master carpenter and a good friend, but Kaylee secretly admitted that his rugged good looks and disarming smile also contributed to her admiration of him.

Kaylee laughed. "I *was* expecting someone else, but you're a welcome surprise."

"Just thought I'd drop in and give you the news in person," Reese said. "Amanda's landlord called me about her back door lock. I just fixed it."

"Oh, good. Did you take a photo of the broken lock first?"

"I thought you might want one." He pulled his phone from his back pocket, found the photo, and showed it to her. "Do you want me to send it to you?"

"Yes. I'll forward it to Amanda's lawyer."

Reese pushed a few buttons, then stuck his phone into his pocket. "I'm not sure it will do her any good," he warned.

"Why not? It's a clear shot." Kaylee glanced outside as the sun passed under a cloud.

"The photo's clear, but it's impossible to tell how recently the lock was damaged. If I were pushed for an answer, I'd say it was probably broken within the last two weeks, but I can't say any closer than that."

Kaylee's shoulders drooped. His news didn't help at all. "So the lock could have been broken even before the theft?"

"The wood around the lock splintered a bit, and the exposed wood underneath hasn't weathered, which suggests a recent break," Reese explained. "But it's in a protected spot under her covered porch, so it wouldn't weather nearly as fast as something exposed to the elements."

Almost as if on cue, a faint rumble to the west reminded Kaylee of the day's forecast. More rain. The humidity and dark days could dampen one's spirits even more than it dampened the ground.

"It sure is quiet in here," Reese remarked.

"It's just me and Bear at the moment. He's napping." She called up the stairs to him.

In seconds the dog flew down the stairs, barking a greeting. Bear raced over to Reese and sniffed his work boots, then lifted his head.

Reese bent down to scratch Bear's ears and straightened his bow tie, which had been knocked crooked by his nap. "Where's Mary?"

Mary Bishop, Kaylee's right hand at The Flower Patch, worked part-time as her floral designer. She knew the meaning of every flower and enjoyed helping people design arrangements that were both beautiful and meaningful. At sixty, she was fit, friendly, and full of energy, a definite asset to the shop.

"She's out of town for a couple of weeks."

"I'm surprised Mary would leave just before the fall festival."

Kaylee smiled at her dog, who trotted back and forth between her and Reese, enjoying the affection he got from both. "It's unusual, yes, but she felt it was important. Mary's college roommate is entering her second marriage after being widowed for many years. Mary's helping her sort out her household so she can move across the country."

"What are the rest of the Petals planning to do at the fall festival?" he asked.

Kaylee and Mary were members of the Petal Pushers garden club, and the group had chosen a charity to work with. "We're raising money for Island Grove, that educational park on the other side of the island."

"That's a great place, and I'm sure they'll appreciate the donation. Are you handling everything all right by yourself?"

"I hired some temporary help. Mary's husband met a man at the library while attending a meeting of his amateur whale watching club."

"Is he a forensic botanist too?" Reese asked, a teasing note in his voice.

Kaylee rolled her eyes. "No, but he can repot plants for the fall festival sale, do some cleaning, and make deliveries."

"And that's enough help?"

"Well, he's not Mary," Kaylee admitted, "but he's been very helpful." She caught movement on the front porch. "Here he is now."

The bell over the door chimed, and Bear barked a greeting.

A man nearing seventy stepped inside. In his neat blue sweater and narrow tie, he was the definition of dapper.

"Good morning, Andrew." Kaylee grinned and waved him closer. "I'd like you to meet our town's master carpenter and handiest handyman, Reese Holt. Reese, this is Andrew Whitaker."

"Glad to meet you." Andrew stuck out his hand. It was thin and covered with leathery, brown skin like the rest of him, including the top of his tanned, nearly bald pate.

Reese shook his hand. "Same here."

Andrew removed his sweater and hung it up, rolled up his shirtsleeves, and smiled at Kaylee. "Where shall I begin today?"

Kaylee handed him a small list on a lavender sticky note shaped like a tulip. "First, start these two arrangements. For one arrangement, let's use *Platycodon grandiflorus*. That's the bluish-purple balloon flower. For the second one, make sure you have room for both the white and blue *Campanula persicifolia*." Andrew nodded. "The peach-leaved bellflower, right?" "Exactly. Can you deliver them when they're done?" "No problem." Andrew headed upstairs to the workroom.

The light from outside dimmed a bit more, and thunder rumbled in the distance. Kaylee saw her hanging baskets of impatiens sway and twist in the wind.

As she hurried to take them down, she asked Reece again, "You're absolutely sure you can't pinpoint when the lock was broken? Surely someone broke in and planted that necklace."

Reese gave her a sheepish expression. "There's one other possibility."

"Like what?"

"I hate to even mention it, but you've told me your friend was short of money."

Kaylee was shocked. "Yes, but Amanda would never steal." How could Reese think what everyone else suspected? And how could he so thoroughly mistrust her judgment?

"What about her daughter?" he asked. "Isn't she in high school?"

"Madison is no more a thief than her mother is," Kaylee said coldly.

"Could the daughter have persuaded a boyfriend to steal it for her? Then he could have delivered it to the house, forced the lock, and hid it in the first place he found before running off."

"No, that's impossible. Madison doesn't even have a boyfriend. Amanda would have told me if she did."

"Parents don't always know," Reese stated.

"True," Kaylee admitted reluctantly. "And Madison is certainly aware of their financial problems."

Just then lightning flashed, thunder boomed, the heavens opened, and rain fell in torrents.

Bear growled deep in his throat.

While Kaylee stroked her trembling dog, she debated Reese's idea, and doubt began to creep in. What if he was right?

If Madison *had* stolen the jewelry—with or without help from a friend—nothing would comfort Amanda, even if she were found innocent herself.

Kaylee was glad to see Madison show up that day after school. She bore a remarkable resemblance to Amanda, except that her blonde, wavy hair sported a short, layered cut.

Every science student had to do something at the high school bazaar to help raise money for new lab equipment, and Madison and her lab partner, Chloe Padgett, planned to sell carnivorous plants such as Venus flytraps, cobra lilies, and sundew plants. They had asked to use the workroom at the flower shop to repot the plants she and Chloe had grown in the biology class's greenhouse. Madison and Kaylee would transfer the seedlings from their trays into individual disposable cups this afternoon.

Madison was positive that kids would buy every plant they had. Kaylee agreed. She herself had always been fascinated with plants that could trap and digest insects.

Kaylee enjoyed Madison's quirky sense of humor, but today, Madison wore a glum expression.

"Mom's at her lawyer's." Madison slumped at the worktable

where the small plants waited alongside a bucket of Kaylee's custom-mixed potting soil—half sand and half peat moss. "Your lawyer will get Mom off, won't he?" Her lower lip trembled, and she bit down on it. "He's really good, right?"

"Yes, Mr. LeMasters is very good, but even a lousy lawyer could get your mother off because she's innocent." Kaylee paused, wanting to cheer Madison up. Maybe the kindest thing to do was to get her mind off her mother—at least for a little while. "What are other kids doing to raise money at the bazaar?"

"Lots of stuff." Madison took a deep breath and straightened. "There's going to be a white elephant auction and a used book sale. Someone's having a photo booth." She shrugged. "There are a few guessing games. You know, like the ones where you guess how many jelly beans or seashells are in a huge jar to get a prize . . ." Her voice trailed off.

Kaylee filled half a dozen of the disposable cups with the loose soil and reached for the tray of cobra lilies. "Some kids from your class were in this week collecting things for a recycling project. They wanted old ink cartridges and flip phones to take to a recycling facility to exchange for cash."

"I think our meat-eating plants are the most unusual idea," Madison said, "but the student art booth will probably make more money."

"Students are selling their art?"

"Yeah. They got their original art printed on mugs and T-shirts. They think they'll sell more that way since the holidays are coming up. The car wash in the parking lot during the bazaar will probably make a lot of cash too."

Kaylee nodded. "It's handy. People can get their cars cleaned while they're inside shopping."

The conversation died off, and Kaylee cast about for other topics of interest to a teenager. Hopefully Andrew would be back soon from his deliveries. To Kaylee's surprise, he and Madison had hit it off earlier.

Kaylee watched Madison out of the corner of her eye as she absentmindedly touched the trigger hair on the edge of a hinged flytrap. It snapped shut, but it would open again in twenty-four hours because there was no food in the trap.

"Oh!" Kaylee said, startling Madison out of her reverie. "I almost forgot. The brochures about the care and feeding of carnivorous plants are done and ready to be proofread and printed. Do you want to go over them with me?"

"Sure." Madison's eyes brightened. "Thanks for designing them."

Kaylee jogged to her office and smiled at Bear curled up in his dog bed for his afternoon siesta. Nothing moved but the gentle rise and fall of his stomach. She grabbed the two designs she'd created. The one on basic care was primarily photos, and the second layout gave more detailed scientific information.

Back in the workroom, Kaylee cleaned spilled potting soil from one end of the worktable and spread out the two brochures side by side. The first one featured large colorful photos of several types of meat-eating plants. Each plant came with a fun fact in a balloon shape. *Venus flytrap jaws snap shut in a tenth of a second. Pitcher plants, also known as cobra lilies, attract insects with a sweet substance in their pitchers. Sundew plants catch insects by wrapping their tentacles around them.*

"What do you think?" Kaylee asked.

Madison held the first brochure up to the light. "This one's good. It's fun, but it also gives enough information at the bottom on how to care for the plants."

"You don't want them to die after buyers take them home."

"Isn't it weird that these plants only grow in poor soil?"

"You just have to match the soil to what they would naturally grow in. Long ago carnivorous plants adapted to nutrient-poor soils that were full of peat and sand," Kaylee explained.

Madison gestured to the bucket of potting soil. "What did you put in it?"

"I used sphagnum peat moss and horticultural sand. The minerals and fertilizer in regular potting soil would kill these little meat eaters." She pointed to the second brochure on the table. "This one is my favorite layout."

Madison picked up the brochure and scanned the blocks of content, then gave Kaylee her first genuine smile of the afternoon. "'*Darlingtonia californica*'?"

"That's your cobra lily." Kaylee's PhD in plant taxonomy had made creating the second brochure enjoyable. It had reminded her of her years as an instructor at the University of Washington in Seattle. "Surely the serious science student wants to know more than a few fun facts. The Venus flytrap is *Dionaea muscipula*. Your sundew plants are the genus *Drosera*, but there are nearly 200 species within that genus. And—"

"Little kids won't read all that," Madison interrupted. "I think it's the elementary and middle school kids who will snap the plants up." She touched a flytrap and made it snap shut. "No pun intended."

Kaylee tried to hide her disappointment. "You don't think they'd want to know more about the botany?"

"Sure, but I think this will be over their heads." Madison read aloud, "'The sundew glands exude nectar, adhesive compounds, and digestive enzymes.' Or this: 'The list of plants described as near carnivorous, protocarnivorous, or borderline carnivorous is quite diverse.'"

"Point taken."

Madison set the brochures down. "Why don't we print seventy-five of the first brochure and maybe twenty of the second one?"

Kaylee tilted her head and studied both layouts. "What if I also add some websites on the bottom of the first brochure so a serious-minded younger student can learn more about the science if he or she wants to?"

The bell over the front door chimed.

A few moments later Andrew appeared in the workroom doorway and waved at Madison, then said to Kaylee, "The rain stopped, and now the sun is out. All the plants have been delivered, and here's the paperwork." He handed over the receipts.

"That's great," Kaylee said as she accepted them. "Thank you."

Andrew turned to Madison. "How's the repotting going?"

Madison beamed and launched into a detailed explanation.

Kaylee smiled, remembering her own times with her grandparents and the wonderful memories they'd shared. Since Madison had no grandparents nearby, Andrew's presence in the shop was an added bonus.

Andrew cleared his throat. "I want to say how sorry I am about your mother. I'm sure this confusion will be cleared up soon."

"Thanks." Madison's voice was almost too soft to hear.

Kaylee hoped Andrew was right, but she wasn't as optimistic. Normally she had confidence in the sheriff's department, but in this case, it didn't seem wise. Not if she wanted to keep Amanda from going to prison.

3

"Madison, would you please take the brochures back to my office before they're completely covered in dirt?" Kaylee asked.

"Sure." Madison hopped down off her stool and left the room.

When Madison was out of earshot, Kaylee said to Andrew, "Thanks for trying to cheer her up. If only we could get to the bottom of this. Apparently, Sheriff Maddox feels their case against Amanda is strong."

"I was thinking about that." Andrew took off his smudged glasses and polished them. "Those jewelry display cases are locked with keys, aren't they? Find out who has access to the keys to those glass cases. Maybe the jewelry was stolen from the cases earlier and no one noticed, so they were never put in the safe at all."

"I hadn't thought of that. It's possible Joseph might not have noticed in his rush to finish the bookwork." Kaylee frowned, considering Andrew's idea. "Naturally Joseph would have a key to the glass cases. Maybe their security guard also knows where a key is kept."

As if by mutual consent, they hushed when Madison returned.

Bear trotted on her heels, refreshed after his nap, and basked in Madison's attention as she petted his silky coat. The dog took up a spot next to Madison's feet when she sat down at the worktable.

The trio spent the next thirty minutes carefully transplanting another twenty delicate pitcher plants. While they worked, Kaylee hardly listened to Madison and Andrew's conversation. Instead, she considered Andrew's idea about the display case keys.

She'd try to follow up on it, but she could easily imagine Sheriff Maddox's response. He wouldn't care if the emerald necklace found in Amanda's kitchen was stolen from a glass case rather than the office safe. Amanda probably knew where the keys were kept. The sheriff would still say she had means and opportunity and the emerald necklace constituted proof.

With a sinking feeling, Kaylee wondered if she had even a slim chance of exposing the real thief and keeping Amanda from prison.

Prison.

Kaylee clenched her fists. She hated to think of Amanda locked up in a prison cell. Kaylee knew from experience the terror and panic that filled such tiny, damp, dark places.

Her musings were interrupted by the chime of the door.

Bear sat up and barked.

"Yoo-hoo!" Penelope called.

"Anyone here?" Sylvia asked.

Kaylee took a shaky breath and brushed off her dirty hands, glad for the arrival of two of her favorite people. "Come on up, ladies!" She checked her watch. It was nearly five thirty already.

Penelope and Sylvia bustled into the workroom, and Bear bounded over to greet them.

Penelope shot Andrew a quizzical glance, then gave Madison a brief hug. "Your dear mother called and said she's held up at the lawyer's office. So we get to take you out for supper. Are you nearly finished?"

"I think so," Madison replied. "Let me clean up the worktable and put these plants in a window."

Andrew cleared his throat quietly.

"Oh, I'm sorry," Kaylee said. "Ladies, I don't believe you've met Andrew Whitaker. He's working part-time to help me get ready for the fall festival while Mary's out of town. Andrew,

Penelope Cole and her sister, Sylvia Rosenthal, own The Chandlery Gift Shop across the street."

"How do you do, ladies?" Andrew asked, his gaze riveted on Penelope.

To Kaylee's surprise and delight, she noticed that Penelope blushed all the way up to her white curls.

Sylvia moved near Kaylee and lowered her voice. "Amanda sounded exhausted on the phone. Has she been working with her lawyer all day?"

"I don't know," Kaylee said. "I suppose it takes a long time to plan a strategy for her defense."

"Are you confident of Mr. LeMasters? We've never used him."

Kaylee nodded. "I don't know how often he argues criminal cases, but I believe—"

"Criminal cases?" Madison sounded near tears. "Mom's no criminal!"

Penelope squeezed Madison's shoulders. "That's not what she meant. A criminal case just means a crime is involved, that's all."

"Well, there might have been a crime, but my mother didn't do it," Madison protested. "I would swear to that on a stack of Bibles."

"We believe you," Andrew said. "And we agree."

Kaylee added her voice to the vote. However, Reese's earlier comments about Madison unwillingly floated back to her.

Could Reese possibly be right? Was Madison so confident that her mother was innocent because she and a friend had done the deed themselves?

No matter how hectic her days were, by the time Kaylee drove the couple of miles out of town to Wildflower Cottage, much of the day's stress had drained from her. Her drive home was lined with mostly firs, cedars, and madrone trees, all evergreen, so the view was much the same year-round. Only the big-leaf maples had turned yellow.

Located in the shadow of Turtleback Mountain, Wildflower Cottage was her dream come true. She pulled into her driveway, grateful as always for her charming white farmhouse, nestled in fields of wild lavender. It was filled with such precious memories of her grandparents.

She parked her red Ford Escape beside the cottage and let herself in the back door, nearly tripping over Bear as he darted between her legs. A hot cup of soothing peppermint tea on the back porch overlooking the lavender fields would take care of any leftover tension of the day.

After putting the kettle on, Kaylee stood at the kitchen window and gazed at Turtleback Mountain. Its majestic height helped shrink her problems down to size.

In the living room, she dropped her purse and keys on an end table, appreciating once again the gleaming wood floors and her cozy hearth. Tonight she would snuggle up with Bear in front of the fire and read. She was anxious to begin another one of Grandpa's mystery novels lined up on the bookshelf he'd made from barn wood. It made her feel close to him again, even though he had passed away years before.

Back in the kitchen, she poured boiling water into a pink mug in the shape of a flowerpot. She was dunking her tea bag when she heard the crunch of gravel in the driveway.

Bear rose up on the windowsill and looked out, then barked joyfully and ran to the door.

Kaylee peeked out the window to see Amanda emerge from her Honda hatchback and stretch.

Amanda resembled a teenager in her billowy flowered shirt

and blue jeans, at least until she drew closer and the strain was visible on her face. Kaylee could see she was exhausted.

Kaylee grabbed another mug and tea bag, then hurried to the front door. "Come on in. I was just making tea. Join me for some on the porch?"

"If you have a few minutes."

"Sure. Where's Madison?"

"With Sylvia and Penelope. I was on my way to pick her up when I thought I'd swing by." Amanda smiled wanly.

Kaylee led the way to the porch. "Let's have a seat," she said, motioning to the pair of white rocking chairs.

They settled into the rockers with their steaming mugs of mint tea.

As if sensing something was wrong, Bear curled up at Amanda's feet.

Kaylee angled her chair to face her friend. Dark circles made Amanda's eyes appear sunken, and blue-green smudges underneath them resembled bruises. She wore her cheerful expression like a mask.

"How are you doing?" Kaylee asked.

Amanda held her mug with both hands, fingers wrapped tightly around it. "To be honest, I don't know. I'm kind of numb. I'm still in shock, I think."

"How did the meeting with Mr. LeMasters go?"

"Okay, I guess. I don't have much experience with this kind of thing to compare to." Amanda forced a laugh, but it fell flat. "He gave me some news, but I don't know if it's good or bad. I'd like your opinion."

"What did he say?"

"That the trial date has been set already. That's good, right?" Amanda asked anxiously. "It'll be over quickly instead of dragging on for months because of a crowded court calendar."

"That's true," Kaylee said. "When is the trial date?"

"In two weeks."

"Two weeks!" Kaylee jerked forward, slopping some hot tea on her jeans. "That is soon."

"It's too soon, isn't it?" Amanda rubbed the back of her neck. "I thought so. They must be convinced they have a strong case against me. Do you suppose they have additional evidence they haven't told the lawyer about?"

"Evidence like what?" Kaylee couldn't think of anything worse than finding one of the stolen necklaces hidden in Amanda's house.

"I don't know. Fake evidence invented by someone? Like whoever planted that necklace in my kitchen. Somehow that necklace ended up in my house."

Amanda sounded in desperate need of encouragement, so Kaylee racked her brain for something positive but true to say. But what could she honestly say? Two weeks surely wasn't adequate time for Amanda's attorney to plan a strategy.

Kaylee pulled her sweater tighter around her. "What did Mr. LeMasters tell you?"

"He says they can't convict because it's all circumstantial. My fingerprints are everywhere, but I worked in the store. I had good reason to be handling the jewelry and touching the safe that day. He's sure they won't convict me."

Kaylee remained silent. She wondered if the attorney was simply giving Amanda false hope. He couldn't really believe that it wouldn't matter that a stolen necklace was found in Amanda's possession.

Amanda reached over and grasped Kaylee's wrist. "How can I ever repay you? I couldn't have afforded a lawyer. And I wonder if a public defender would put much effort into building a defense."

"You have nothing to repay me for." In the lengthening shadows, Kaylee studied her friend's weary expression.

Amanda glanced at her watch in the light spilling out from the windows of the cottage. "I'd better get moving. I'll call Madison and tell her I'm on the way. Thanks for letting me de-stress."

"Anytime."

Amanda picked up her phone and teacup and headed inside to make her call.

Kaylee watched her go. She wouldn't add to Amanda's worries for the world, but in her heart of hearts, she believed that if something significant wasn't discovered before the trial, Amanda would go to prison.

And as desperately as she wanted to stop that from happening, Kaylee feared there wasn't a thing she could do.

4

Kaylee and Bear slipped inside the house as Amanda was hanging up. She wore the first genuine smile that Kaylee had seen in days.

"Madison sounded well. They've just finished eating homemade chicken and noodles and peach pie. Now they're playing dominoes."

"Good, I'm glad." That sounded like a vast improvement over Madison's somber mood at the shop earlier. "I don't know how much time you'll need to spend with Mr. LeMasters working on your case, but when you're free, I'd love to have your help at the shop."

"Really?"

"Absolutely. With Mary gone, I haven't had time to do any crafts for the Petal Pushers for the fall festival bazaar. I've only been keeping up with orders because of Andrew. We're making crafts out of fall flowers, flint corn, dried grasses, you name it."

The Petal Pushers focused on socializing as much as gardening, and Kaylee loved that. She'd become an automatic member when her grandmother had sold her The Flower Patch. The club regularly met in the Old Cape Lighthouse's keeper's quarters to work on various projects.

Amanda poured her cold tea in the sink and rinsed the cup. "If you show me what to do, I'll do my best on whatever crafts you need."

Kaylee tapped her fingernail against her mug. "One thing we're making is corn-husk dolls of various sizes. I ordered the corn husks online, and a huge box of them arrived today. I put the corn husks in a tub of water to soak. They'll need to be trimmed and then bagged up to stay supple."

"I could do that," Amanda said. "Is it okay if I start Monday? I promised Madison a trip to the mainland tomorrow. I thought we both needed some time away."

"That's perfect. Come in on Monday and any other time that Mr. LeMasters doesn't need to meet with you. Madison plans to come after school next week to work on her carnivorous plant project."

Amanda gave Kaylee a hug that nearly squeezed the breath out of her. "What would I do without you?"

Kaylee didn't answer. She knew exactly what Amanda would have done without her. She'd have stayed living on the mainland instead of living in Turtle Cove facing a jail term.

On Monday morning Amanda was already waiting at The Flower Patch when Kaylee arrived.

Bear leaped from the car and greeted Amanda.

She stooped and scratched Bear's back. "My, how handsome you are today in your blue bow tie."

Bear's ears perked up, and he sat straighter, giving Amanda a better view of his finery.

Kaylee laughed. "Bear, stop preening." She opened the shop and turned on the lights. "How was your day on the mainland?"

"It was relaxing. Just what the doctor ordered for both of us."

"That's wonderful." Kaylee gestured toward the back wall of hooks. "You can leave your coat and purse there, and then I'll show you what to do with this tub of soaked corn husks."

Amanda shed her jacket and hung it up along with her purse.

Kaylee squeezed Amanda's arm. "You're a godsend. I've felt guilty about not contributing my part to the Petal Pushers, but with Mary gone . . ." She shrugged. "You'll be my second pair of hands."

"I'll do what I can," Amanda said, pushing up her sleeves.

"We'll have the place to ourselves this morning. My part-time help, Andrew, comes in after lunch today. He repotted plants with Madison after school too."

"I look forward to meeting him. Madison really likes him."

"Watching them, you'd almost think she's his granddaughter. Let's get started." She led the way upstairs to the workroom.

Bear followed, making a beeline for his bed in Kaylee's office.

Kaylee lifted a blue plastic tub to the worktable. "I confess that I'm not terribly crafty, so if my doll ends up resembling a moose more than a man, I'll just dispose of it and trust you to keep my secret."

Amanda laughed. "Give me the instructions. Surely between the two of us we can figure it out."

They gathered string, scissors, the soaked corn husks, and printed diagrams for making both the boy and girl dolls. For the next hour, Kaylee and Amanda worked side by side. Kaylee followed the directions for a boy doll while Amanda created a girl doll. During the first several steps, both dolls looked the same.

"Homely little guys, aren't they?" Amanda chuckled as she regarded her bunched-up corn husks.

After arranging four pliable corn husks with the pointed ends down, they used small pieces of string to tie the flat ends tightly together. Then they trimmed around the edges, arranged the corn husks with the pointy sides up, and folded the long ends of the husks down over the trimmed edges.

"Oh, I see what we're doing." Amanda pointed at her corn husks. "This part's going to be the head."

Kaylee frowned at her own lumpy ball of corn husk compared to the smooth ball Amanda had created. She didn't see what Amanda apparently did. "If you say so," she said dubiously.

Amanda pored over the instructions. "Next, lay your doll head and body aside. Grab a separate wide piece of corn husk and roll it up this way, like a cigar. Good. Now hold the ends, and I'll tie them so they don't unroll."

A minute later, Amanda grinned. "See? It makes arms, and the tied-off ends are the little hands. You stick this 'cigar' through the doll body under the head so the arms stick out on both sides."

"I'll take your word for it." Kaylee shook her head. "I don't understand. I put together plants and flowers and rocks and bits of wood to make lovely arrangements, if I do say so myself. So why am I all thumbs with this stuff? Some pioneer mother I would have made."

"You're too hard on yourself." Amanda paused and examined her half-finished doll. "Thanks again for asking me to help. The days drag when I'm alone and I have too much time to think."

"I'm glad you decided to give it a try." Kaylee held up her own doll, which was starting to come apart. "Now what?"

Amanda tilted her head and studied it. "You didn't do the shoulders part. You need to put a husk around the arms and upper body—like mine—in a crisscross pattern to make shoulders."

Kaylee tried again, but she still couldn't get it right.

Amanda watched her for a moment. "Here, let me help smooth it down. You don't want him to look like some kind of bodybuilder."

Amanda didn't bother giving the boy doll back to Kaylee after that. Instead, she deftly tied off the hanging corn husks into two legs and feet, then cut off the excess. For her girl doll, Amanda gathered four of the hanging corn husks and trimmed them, then spread them out to create a long skirt.

"Ta-da!" She gathered up the dolls and, with them facing each other, danced them across the worktable.

"Well done." Kaylee grinned. "You've found your niche. I'll leave you to make the dolls while I put together a get-well arrangement that was ordered online this morning. That is, if you don't mind."

"Of course not. You do your thing, and I'll do mine."

They chatted while Kaylee gathered fresh-cut red roses, pink roses, pink lilies, and purple wax flowers. They would go in a clear glass vase decorated with a pink ribbon. When finished, it would measure about fourteen inches high.

She hummed as she worked, snipping the stems at an angle so they'd take in more water. She arranged the roses first to get the lengths staggered just right. First the light pink *Rosa canina*, then the brighter pink *Rosa carolina*, and the red *Rosa chinensis* with its fuller shape. Two delicate pink *Lilium japonicum* would fill out the bouquet with both elegance and their heady scent.

Kaylee debated about the wax flowers and finally decided against them. It was important to know when to stop, and the purple felt too jarring with the colors she already had.

Kaylee and Amanda worked in companionable silence. Kaylee's playlist of her favorite eighties music resonated softly in the background, and she smiled at Amanda singing along with Stevie Wonder's "I Just Called to Say I Love You." They followed that with a dramatic duet of Bonnie Tyler's "Total Eclipse of the Heart."

Stretching to get the kinks out of her back and neck, Kaylee counted Amanda's finished dolls, glad again that she'd asked for her assistance.

Kaylee had finished her get-well arrangement and was ready to make a bouquet for a baby girl. She loved making arrangements to send to new mothers. While she appreciated the genuine value of flowers for the sick and bereaved, it was pure joy to create bouquets to celebrate newborns.

Mary had taught her the meaning or the "language" for many of the flowers they used, and Kaylee named them under her breath as she chose stems from various buckets of cut flowers. "Lily of the valley, purity of heart. White roses, a new beginning. Pink carnations, a mother's love." Kaylee liked to use carnations whenever she could. Besides giving off a wonderful long-lasting scent, she could include five carnations for the price of a single rose.

Tapping her foot to the music, Kaylee positioned the lamb flower holder, its sweet face making her smile. Then she tied pink and white lace ribbons around the lamb's neck. It was the perfect finishing touch.

Twice while she worked, she had to pause to assist customers off the street.

Mrs. Anderson wanted a brown, orange, and gold house-warming arrangement for her daughter and son-in-law. Kaylee grinned as Mrs. Anderson tried to corral her grandson, keeping one arm wrapped around him so he couldn't get away. The toddler stomped his solid chubby legs and scattered handfuls of cereal from a plastic bag.

Kaylee had no sooner picked up after him and gone back to the workroom than a fiftyish woman swooped into the shop looking for lavender and lilac soaps and lotions. She was as stringy as a long-distance runner, and she wore thick popcorn socks and well-worn sneakers.

Each time Kaylee returned to the worktable, Amanda was still working with the corn husks. In addition to finishing a dozen dolls, she'd filled a large number of individual plastic bags with soaked and trimmed corn husks, ready to be crafted into dolls of various sizes.

Kaylee finished a white-and-gold mum arrangement and placed it in the cooler for Andrew to deliver later. She rejoined Amanda in the workroom and wiped her hands on her jeans. "Would you like to see the brochures I designed for Madison's carnivorous plants?"

"Sure." Amanda set a bundle of soaked corn husks back into the tub of water and reached for a towel. "Let me dry off."

"No need. I'll run into my office and grab them." Kaylee was searching for the brochures when she heard the bell sound over the front door. *Busy morning.* Her phone rang at the same time.

Amanda called out, "I'll get the door!"

"Thanks!" Kaylee grabbed the phone. It was an excited daughter planning a retirement party for her father. She wanted to nail down a delivery time to make sure someone would be around when the flowers were delivered.

After Kaylee hung up, she scribbled a few notes on her pad of paper. She turned to find Amanda slumped in the office doorway, her eyes downcast. Kaylee's heart skipped a beat. "What is it?"

"There's a Mrs. Johnson in the shop who wants—no, is demanding—to talk to you."

5

Kaylee studied Amanda's stricken face. "What's wrong?"

When Amanda didn't answer, Kaylee's pulse quickened. She gently took Amanda by the wrist. "What's the matter?"

Amanda hesitated. "I'm fine," she said unconvincingly. "But you'd better get down there."

She'd find out what was wrong with her friend after she'd handled this customer. Kaylee rushed downstairs.

A scowling woman dressed in a black coat stood stiffly near the display of potted gold, lavender, and bronze chrysanthemums.

Kaylee smiled. "May I help you, Mrs. Johnson? I'm Kaylee Bleu. I don't believe we've met."

"No, but I knew your grandmother." Nose in the air, Mrs. Johnson stared at her through the bottom half of her bifocals. "She'd come back to Turtle Cove like a shot if she knew you had a criminal working in her beautiful store."

Kaylee gasped and glanced over her shoulder, hoping fervently that Amanda had stayed upstairs and not overheard that remark. "You must be mistaken." Her smile felt stiff, but she kept it firmly in place. "There are no criminals here."

The woman snorted and pulled her coat more closely around her. "I know who that woman is. Her picture's in the newspaper for robbing a jewelry store."

"She was unjustly accused," Kaylee replied, "and I'm sure she'll be vindicated soon."

Mrs. Johnson sniffed as if she smelled something spoiled. "In the meantime, I would keep her out of sight. If your customers spot her working here, you'll lose business, including mine."

With that, she spun on the heel of her boot and marched out the door, slamming it behind her.

What a nasty, rude woman. Shaking with fury, Kaylee turned and headed back toward the stairs.

Amanda stood there, hugging herself. "I'm so sorry. I never thought—"

"Don't worry about her. Really." Kaylee gritted her teeth. "That crank doesn't represent most people in Turtle Cove."

"I hope not." Amanda chewed her lower lip. "Even so, I should stay out of sight from now on."

Kaylee nodded. "It might be best. I don't want you dealing with another mean customer."

"And I don't want to affect your business more than I already have when you've been so kind to me."

Kaylee hugged her friend tightly, then peered into her eyes. "I'm not worried about my business. I just want your innocence proven."

They returned to work, but the shine had gone off the morning. Kaylee hated that Amanda needed to hide to avoid being humiliated. That hadn't been her intention when she'd invited Amanda to spend time at The Flower Patch.

She glanced at Amanda out of the corner of her eye, dismayed by the dejected slump of her shoulders.

Kaylee reached for her phone in her back pocket and sent a quick text. A minute later, her phone dinged. She read the message and said to Amanda, "It's all set. Let's go for a short drive."

At the word *drive*, Bear jumped up and trotted back and forth between Kaylee and Amanda, then stood up against Kaylee's leg, staring at her eagerly.

Kaylee smiled and scratched behind his ears.

"A drive?" Amanda asked.

Kaylee pointed to two small sturdy boxes. "You've trimmed

and bagged a lot of the corn husks, plenty for the Petal Pushers to also make some dolls. Let's take what you've done down to the lighthouse. Both Jessica Roberts and DeeDee Wilcox will be there. You can show them how to make the dolls. Since Mary and I aren't able to help with the crafts, I know they'll welcome your willing hands."

"But I'm not an official Petal. Don't you have to be invited to join?"

"Yes, but I'm asking you to sub for me. The Petals meet in the Old Cape Lighthouse's keeper's quarters. People like Mrs. Johnson won't barge in off the street and harass you."

Amanda smiled wryly. "Then I shouldn't embarrass anyone there."

Kaylee bit her tongue. Mrs. Johnson's behavior wasn't her fault, but she wished she knew how to make things right.

Kaylee picked up one of the lightweight boxes of corn husks, and Amanda grabbed the other one. Bear led the way downstairs.

Kaylee stuck her *Back in 30 Minutes* sign in the front window and snapped Bear's leash on his collar. The lighthouse was near the flower shop, but after Amanda's run-in with Mrs. Johnson, parading down Main Street together didn't seem like a wise choice. They'd take the car.

Stretching his leash to the last inch, Bear ran ahead and barked, then lagged behind Kaylee to examine insects on the sidewalk.

"Come on, Bear. Keep up." Kaylee unlocked her car, ushered him inside, and set the boxes of corn husks on the back seat.

A few minutes later as they pushed open the door to the lighthouse, they found it had been transformed into a craft shop. The main room held four card tables covered with miniature ears of flint corn, candles of all sizes, dried grasses, orange bittersweet, and ribbons of orange, yellow, and russet.

Kaylee and Amanda set their boxes down, and Kaylee unsnapped Bear from his leash.

Bear scampered over to Jessica who sat at one of the tables. She was creating a wreath from small ears of flint corn, and she paused in her work to give him an affectionate back scratch. The yellow, dark red, and purple ears pointed to the center of the wreath, and the bleached husks were pulled back to flare out around the wreath, like the rays of the sun.

"Those are beautiful," Kaylee said. "They should make good money for Island Grove. If you have any left over from the festival, I'll sell them in my shop." She waved Amanda in from where she hesitated in the doorway. "Amanda, you remember Jessica Roberts. She owns Death by Chocolate, the bakery next to my shop."

Amanda smiled tentatively. "Hello again."

Jessica, a petite Japanese-American woman, beamed at her, then sneezed three times in quick succession. "Sorry. My allergies are acting up." She blew her nose. "I certainly remember you and your lovely daughter from when you've been in the bakery."

Amanda smiled broader. "Madison and I love your shop, especially the mousse meringues. They're so light and delicious. I could eat half a dozen in one sitting."

"I'm partial to her fudge truffles myself," said the woman with the blonde, sun-streaked hair. She was decorating candleholders with dried flowers, corn husks, and tiny sprigs of bittersweet. "I'm DeeDee Wilcox."

"Hi," Amanda said. "You own the mystery bookstore, right?"

"Guilty as charged."

Kaylee grinned as Bear bounded over to DeeDee and reveled in her attention. "In addition to running Between the Lines, DeeDee also makes those lovely herbal soaps in my shop."

"Madison loves your lavender soap," Amanda said.

DeeDee smiled. "It's always nice to hear when your work is appreciated. But I enjoy it so much that it doesn't even feel like work."

Kaylee opened her cardboard box. "We brought you some corn husks that have been soaked overnight, then trimmed. Each bag holds enough to make one doll."

"Fantastic." Jessica pulled up another folding chair. "Get comfortable, and show me what you brought. I've been itching to start the corn-husk dolls." She fingered a bag of pliable corn husks. "Thanks for doing the prep work."

"I can't take credit for any of it. While I worked on flower arrangement orders this morning, Amanda trimmed and bagged everything here." Kaylee snapped her fingers. "Rats. I forgot to grab one of your finished dolls, Amanda."

"That's all right. They're easy, and I've made enough to have them memorized," Amanda said, unpacking her own box. "Tell me again where the proceeds are going."

"It's called the Island Grove charity foundation." Jessica sneezed, then grabbed another tissue to blow her nose. "Island Grove is on the eastern side of Orcas Island. It's a 250-acre outdoor learning center for both children and adults."

"You learn all about environmental stewardship of the island," DeeDee added. "They have a huge volunteer program for cleaning the streams and maintaining the trails. Sometimes I volunteer in the plant nursery."

"The place is impressive," Kaylee agreed. "My favorite areas are the garden beds. They're designed to emphasize certain tastes, colors, and smells." She patted Bear's head, then pointed toward the welcome mat. He obediently trotted over and lay down on it. "They even have tasting tours so people can appreciate what fresh produce tastes like, without it being encased in plastic or canned."

"I'll have to take Madison there sometime," Amanda said. "I can see why you chose that particular charity. It sounds like a worthy cause."

Jessica counted the bags of soft, damp corn husks. "There's enough here for two dozen dolls or more." She grinned at Amanda. "Now, can you stay and help make them?"

Kaylee breathed a sigh of relief at Jessica's enthusiastic invitation. But when DeeDee didn't chime in, Kaylee turned to her in confusion.

DeeDee stared out the window and scanned the street. Her forehead was puckered into a slight frown.

Kaylee leaned closer to get a better view but spotted nothing unusual outside. "DeeDee?" she whispered. "Are you okay?"

DeeDee whipped around. "I'm sorry. My mind was wandering for a minute." She glanced across the room where Jessica and Amanda were already creating two corn-husk dolls and laughing at some of the instructions. DeeDee lowered her voice. "We don't need to take your helper from you. With Mary gone, you must be swamped."

Kaylee studied DeeDee's ambivalent expression. Was that a hint to take Amanda back to The Flower Patch with her? Why? Amanda's presence couldn't bother anyone here.

"It's settled," Jessica called. She sneezed again and apologized. "I'm keeping Amanda here to work on the corn-husk dolls. She even offered to make some little aprons and bonnets for the mama dolls."

"That is, if you don't mind." Amanda raised a quizzical eyebrow at Kaylee. "I haven't finished bagging all the corn husks yet."

"That can wait until you're ready for more. The corn husks need to stay moist and pliable anyway, so they're easier to work with."

"Good." Jessica stood and stretched. "I need a break. Can I coax you into a chocolate muffin and coffee?"

"I'd love to, but I have to get back to the shop." Kaylee grabbed Bear's leash and snapped it on. "See you all later."

Amid the flurry of goodbyes, Kaylee couldn't help but notice that DeeDee still appeared distracted, even nervous.

Outside, Kaylee climbed into her car and sat motionless. "What do you think is wrong with DeeDee?" she asked Bear. Clearly something about Amanda was bothering her. But she'd been perfectly friendly toward her when Kaylee and Amanda had first arrived.

Did DeeDee know something the rest of them didn't?

Kaylee was parking near The Flower Patch when she saw Joseph step outside the jewelry store. He appeared to be checking the placement of a sign in his front window. Despite Bear's tug on his leash, she strode right past the flower shop and across the street.

"Mr. Liddon!" she called out. "Do you have a minute?"

At the sight of her, Joseph's welcoming smile melted into suspicion. He gazed down at Bear with undisguised disgust.

Bear appeared to return the sentiment. There was something about the store owner that Bear didn't like, and Kaylee thought it showed Bear's excellent judgment of character. Or maybe he sensed Joseph's jealousy. After all, Bear's starched cobalt-blue bow tie was far more dashing than Joseph's limp brown one.

"You're Mrs. Denman's friend," Joseph huffed.

"Yes, Kaylee Bleu. I own The Flower Patch."

"You interfered when the police were here."

Kaylee blinked at the accusation. "I care about Amanda, and I want to help get to the bottom of this if I can."

"There's nothing you can do, unless it's to persuade your friend to return my jewelry."

Kaylee refused to take his bait. As much as it depended on her, she'd get along with Joseph. "Can we please go over what happened on the evening of the robbery? I want to get some things clear in my mind."

"The police have my statement, and I have nothing new to add. Now please excuse me." Joseph started back inside.

Kaylee called after him, "Amanda is innocent! Someone else stole those jewels. Why won't you admit that it's at least a possibility?"

Three people on the sidewalk stopped and stared.

Bear gave a low growl meant to intimidate, and Kaylee patted him for his effort.

"You're making a spectacle of yourself out here," Joseph said, tightening his jaw.

"We could talk inside then."

Joseph glanced at the staring shoppers who strolled by in slow motion. "I'll give you five minutes. I'm a very busy man."

Inside The Velvet Box, a new clerk was showing wedding ring sets to a young couple. It was all Kaylee could do not to scowl at Amanda's replacement.

The only other customer was a tall man half hidden behind a pillar. In his gray three-piece suit, light pink shirt, and dark pink tie, he looked more like a high-fashion mannequin than the average Turtle Cove shopper. A rich mannequin too, judging by the large diamond ring and his watch encircled with diamonds. *And he has the most remarkable light blue eyes.*

The new clerk motioned to Joseph, so he went over to talk to her.

While Kaylee waited, she kept Bear's leash tight, and he sat at her feet. She scanned the glass display cases filled with tastefully displayed jewelry: rings, necklaces, pendants, and bracelets. Displays of less expensive watches rotated slowly while the designer watches gleamed in their locked display case.

Kaylee turned at Joseph's approach. "What I wanted to ask—"

"Not here," Joseph interrupted. "In my office."

Before Kaylee could follow him, the tall man stepped out from behind the pillar. "Excuse me. Are you the owner?"

Joseph looked him up and down, and his irritated expression transformed into an ingratiating smile. "Yes. How can I help you?"

"I work for an upmarket retailer, and I'm interested in investing, particularly in ruby and emerald necklaces."

Kaylee stepped back, wondering what Joseph would do if she piped up with the suggestion that the investor stop at the sheriff's office if he was interested in emeralds.

Joseph frowned slightly. "You're an investor?"

"Yes. Investing in the right jewelry is like investing in a beautiful piece of artwork," he said smoothly.

Joseph nodded slowly as he studied the man before him.

"Excuse me. I should have given you my card." He pulled a business card from a leather case and handed it to Joseph. "I'm Michael Scott. I work out of the San Francisco office, but our headquarters are in Paris."

Joseph scanned the card, then glanced at Kaylee in annoyance. "I have something to attend to, but it will take only a few minutes. If you don't mind waiting?"

"No problem," the investor said. "I'll continue to browse."

The plush maroon carpet muffled Kaylee's steps as she and Bear followed Joseph down a hallway to a small office near the rear exit. She searched for an escape route in case she needed to leave quickly. Did that door open on the alley? She felt childish, but her heart was beating like a trapped bird.

Kaylee glanced around the tiny office. It was tidy, with expensive wooden furniture and several family photos in silver frames on the shelves.

Joseph stood behind his polished mahogany desk, a ledger

open on it. "Close the door behind you." His tone was flat, the words clipped.

The hairs on Kaylee's arms stood up. Bear scuttled behind her and pressed his nose against the back of her leg. He peeked out as if trying to decide whether it was safe to emerge.

"What do you want?" Joseph demanded. "As you know, I have pressing things to attend to."

"I heard what you and Amanda said to the sheriff, and it struck me as odd that your stories were the same, yet Amanda was charged with the theft. She never denied that she put the last of the necklaces in the safe and twirled the knob of the combination lock to lock it. You both agreed that you told her to do that while you finished some paperwork at your desk here."

"Correct." He rocked back and forth on the balls of his feet. "However, I never told her to help herself to some of the jewelry *before* she locked the safe."

"Did you see any such thing?" Kaylee asked.

"That's hardly necessary. Given the fact that the emerald necklace was found at Mrs. Denman's home, it is self-evident." He leaned over his desk toward her, palms flat on top of his ledger. "At least the police think so."

"Until this incident," Kaylee said, "how would you describe Amanda's work for you?"

Joseph's chest deflated. His bulging froggy eyes even seemed to sink back into his head. "Actually, she was one of the best employees I've ever had. She was good with customers, punctual, and always stayed busy."

"Trustworthy?"

"I thought so, but this was the first time I trusted her to lock the safe for me. I'm very disappointed in her. Apparently, the temptation was too strong."

"I don't believe that."

"It matters very little what you think."

Kaylee bristled at the remark, but she couldn't really argue with the truth of it. "Who else has access to your safe or maybe keys to your glass display cases?"

"No one."

"No one at all? What about after hours? You have a cleaning crew, don't you?"

"A janitor, Ronald Borton."

"What about security—a night watchman?"

"Thomas Rider is a security guard for us and several other Turtle Cove stores."

"Well, what about them? Couldn't one of those men be your thief?"

"There was no sign of tampering with the safe, no keys missing, and no glass cases broken."

"Then how can you say Amanda is guilty?" Kaylee persisted.

"I never claimed Mrs. Denman broke into the safe. I believe she either took the jewelry *before* she locked the safe, or she watched me enough times as I opened the safe in the morning that she figured out the combination. She was always nearby while I opened up."

"What?" Kaylee's voice almost squeaked. How could he have been that careless with anyone? "You let her stand right beside you while you opened the safe?"

"No, of course not," Joseph barked. "But a few quick glances, a glimpse here and there as she walked by, and over time she could have worked out the numbers I was using."

Bear edged out from behind Kaylee and sniffed. She bent and gave him a reassuring pat, then stood again. "But why now? Why would Amanda jeopardize her job, her life, and her daughter's life by doing such a thing?"

"Why does anyone commit a crime?" he replied. "They think the reward outweighs the risk."

"Amanda's not like that."

"Maybe you don't know your friend as well as you think you do. As I told the sheriff, when Mrs. Denman's thirty-day probationary period was up last week, she asked me for a raise. Business has slowed down with the tourist season about over, and I had to refuse." Joseph shrugged. "She was apparently more desperate for money than I realized."

Kaylee pressed her lips together. She knew Amanda's financial situation was tight, but it was news to her that she'd asked for a raise and been denied. And the sheriff knew too.

He checked the clock on his desk. "Is that all?"

"Just one more thing. Who locks the front and back doors at closing time?"

"I lock the front door at six o'clock on most nights, but the back door that opens onto the alley is kept locked during the day as well."

"All the time?" Kaylee could picture a thief sneaking in the back door, hiding in a storeroom or a broom closet until the store was locked up at night, then coming out of hiding to rob the safe.

"The back door is locked during the day," he explained. "The night security guard checks both doors, front and back, several times during the night when he makes the rounds."

"How do you know?"

"Because that's what I pay him for." Joseph sighed. "Look, I understand you want to help your friend, but you're not a policewoman." He waved her away. "Go back to picking flowers and leave this to the professionals."

Kaylee chafed at both his patronizing words and tone, but she refused to let him see that his words had hit the mark.

"You can go out the back door." He glanced down at Bear with obvious distaste. "No need to parade him through my store again."

Without a backward glance, Kaylee left through the rear exit. She closed the door behind her and heard the automatic lock click into place. *So much for that theory.*

While Bear wound his leash around her ankles, Kaylee used her phone's note-taking app to record Joseph's comments while they were still fresh in her mind.

She frowned as she slid her phone into her back pocket. She couldn't put her finger on it, but something Joseph had said jarred her. But what?

6

Back at The Flower Patch, Kaylee checked her watch and gasped. Nearly eleven! It was only Monday, and she was already falling behind.

And she hadn't even begun to put together her largest fall festival orders. The most challenging one was the giant arrangement for Nora Keller, the artist who owned Art Attack. Her gallery on Main Street featured original paintings, framed photos, sculptures, and high-end Native American art.

The day before the jewelry robbery, Nora had popped into The Flower Patch and unrolled a folded sketch on the counter, her green eyes sparkling and long blonde braid swinging. Dressed in a paint-splattered shirt, faded jeans, and red tennis shoes, she looked more like a high school art student than a successful entrepreneur in her thirties.

"I want the arrangement like this," she'd explained, indicating the sketch, "and I want it big. Five or six feet tall."

"Where do you plan to put it?" Kaylee had asked. "And give me an idea of what colors you want to use."

"It will go on a table just inside the store. It's going to be a fall festival raffle gift." She tapped the paper. "And I want it to be all white."

Kaylee enjoyed a challenge, but it had taken a couple of days to wrap her mind around the idea. But it grew on her as she assembled what Nora wanted. It would include miniature gourds and pumpkins painted white, a dozen white votive candles, bleached Hokitika driftwood pieces, white shells, and a dozen peace lilies. The satiny white *Spathiphyllum wallisii* waited in a bucket of water in the cooler.

She'd also promised a set of four floral bouquets for Olivia Thomas at The Chic Boutique. In her forties, Olivia was excellent advertising for her boutique, and her fashionable clothing could make Kaylee feel frumpy if she let it. Olivia wanted her fall festival arrangements to have hollowed-out pumpkins for vases, filled with purple and russet mums, sunflowers, and bulrushes.

Kaylee had tried to talk Olivia into letting her use artificial pumpkins for vases so the arrangements would last longer and not have to be created at the last minute. But Olivia insisted on real pumpkins because they needed to last only a few days for the festival.

Joseph's caustic remarks reverberated in Kaylee's mind as she gathered materials for Nora's all-white arrangement. She'd already spray-painted the gourds and pumpkins white, with several coats of paint to cover the blemishes.

Bear followed her back and forth while she worked. Soon the dog yawned and dragged his feet, then retired to his bed in her office for a nap.

Andrew would come in at noon, and with luck, the customers would hold off and give her some uninterrupted work time. How she missed Mary on days like this.

She closed her eyes, took several deep breaths, and deliberately smiled. It was amazing how a big smile lifted her spirits, even when she didn't feel cheerful. She'd read somewhere that the act of smiling—even for no reason at all—actually raised a person's serotonin levels and lowered the stress hormone, cortisol.

Humming, Kaylee headed for the closet under the stairs to dig out the smooth driftwood pieces she'd ordered from New Zealand. Completely white, the wood would make an excellent sturdy base for the large arrangement. She flicked on the overhead light in the closet. It flashed on, and then with a small *pop*, it went out.

Oh, for heaven's sake. Why did light bulbs burn out at the most inconvenient times?

She could run upstairs to the cupboard in her office and get a new one, but she was pretty sure where she had stashed the box of driftwood when it was delivered. It was tucked behind an arbor draped with tulle and strung with fairy lights that she'd recently used for a wedding. She moved boxes of florist foam, packs of gold and silver wire, boxes of orange and yellow silk flowers, and glass marbles used for vase fillers. She crawled on her hands and knees beneath the stairs, feeling more than seeing in the dark closet.

Now where was that box of driftwood? Maybe she'd have to fetch a new light bulb after all.

While Kaylee was backing out on her hands and knees, the closet door slammed shut, plunging her into total darkness. She froze for a split second. Suddenly she was five years old again and terrified of the dark.

Her heart skipped a beat, and blood thundered so loud in her ears that she could hear nothing else. She crouched in the blackness, motionless for what felt like several minutes but was probably no more than ten seconds. *Get me out of here!*

Kaylee scrambled to the door and shoved on it as hard as she could. It stuck fast, swollen from the recent rains. Panic seized her, and she knew she was hyperventilating. She gripped the knob and twisted, but nothing happened. Pushing again, she leaned her shoulder hard into the door.

She closed her eyes and screamed, "Help! I'm in here!"

The door flew open, and she landed at Andrew's feet.

"Miss Bleu!" Andrew reached down and grasped Kaylee's arm to help her up. "Are you all right? I didn't know anyone was in there."

Kaylee laughed, feeling foolish. Standing, she brushed off

the dirt on her knees. "I was trying to find a box of driftwood under the stairs. The light bulb burned out, and I was too lazy to change the bulb."

"I didn't know you were in there," Andrew repeated. "I'm very sorry."

"No problem." She closed the closet door lightly. "It will be nice when the humidity drops enough for the doors to stop sticking."

"These old buildings are notorious for that. Have you had the doors and window frames resealed lately?"

Kaylee blinked. "No, never."

"Do you know when that was last done?"

"I don't know if Grandma ever did it or not. Are you supposed to?"

"Many people who live near water where the humidity's high have them resealed regularly."

Kaylee sighed. One more thing to do. But not today. She had to get back to work.

Andrew started dusting the displays of soaps. Kaylee grinned. He was a sight to see, a nearly seventy-year-old man in blue suspenders brandishing a feather duster.

After retrieving the driftwood and grabbing dried cranberries and roasted almonds to snack on, Kaylee went upstairs to the workroom. The store remained quiet, and soon the giant arrangement for Art Attack began to come together.

When the shop bell chimed, Kaylee swallowed quickly, brushed off her hands, and hurried downstairs. Reese and Andrew were laughing about something.

Feeling betrayed by their laughter, Kaylee bristled. "Did Andrew tell you about my panic attack after getting stuck in a closet?"

Andrew looked aghast. "I wouldn't gossip about you."

Reese raised an eyebrow. "What's all this about?" he asked after Andrew walked off to clean out the coolers.

"Nothing." Kaylee wasn't in the mood to admit to a childhood trauma that she thought had been buried long ago but obviously still had a grip on her. "A few doors stick and won't close right. Then when they do close, they won't open. I got stuck in the closet for a minute."

"Do you want me to check it out?" Reese asked.

"Thanks, but I'm sure you didn't drop in for that. Can I help you with something?"

"No, I was headed to the mainland to pick up some supplies. I only stopped to see if you needed anything. Do you want to show me the door while I'm here?" Reese grinned. "Have hammer, will travel."

"If you have time." Kaylee showed him the closet door. "This one isn't as important, but the back door leading outside is swollen too. I really have to shove it to make the latch catch properly."

Reese tested the doors, running his hands all around the edges and the frames.

"I suppose you either have to sand down the doors or the doorframes," she said, "then reseal everything."

"First things first. Everyone on the island has this trouble after a humid summer. There are some quick fixes for sticky doors, depending on how bad they are."

"Like what?"

"A circulating fan aimed at the door can reduce humidity and the swelling. Or a blow dryer. Just don't burn the wood." Reese pointed to several places. "Where the doors stick the worst, you can lubricate with a bar of soap or some wax to get you through the most humid times."

"Okay, I'll try out those ideas."

"I also checked the hinges—they're still tight. Sometimes screws in the hinges get loose so the doors sag enough to stick." He jammed his hands into his back pockets. "If the quick fixes don't work for you, I can take the doors down later and sand them."

She froze, thinking about something he had said.

"Kaylee?"

She startled. "I'm sorry. What?"

Reese laughed. "I know this isn't the most fascinating subject, but where were you?"

"You said everyone has this problem after a humid summer," Kaylee said. "Do you suppose this could have happened to the jewelry store's back door? Maybe when the night watchman checked the doors on his rounds, he didn't realize the door was just stuck but not actually latched or locked. Does that sound possible?"

"Maybe," Reese admitted, but he looked doubtful. "But could they set the security alarm if the door wasn't actually shut tight? I can't with the system I have at my house. This chirpy voice pipes up and says, 'Garage door open' or 'Sliding door open.'"

Kaylee shrugged. "Has anyone checked the background of the security guy? He could pretend the door was locked when he knew it was only stuck and *claim* he set the alarm. Then he could come back during his rounds in the middle of the night and go into the store, undisturbed and undetected."

Reese frowned. "But wouldn't Joseph set the alarm when he closed the store?"

"Probably. But who has the code? The security firm must have the codes for when the alarms go off. Would the security guard know the codes too?"

Before Reese could answer, the bell over the front door chimed, and Amanda entered the shop.

Kaylee hoped the Petal Pushers had been productive today so she could display a selection of corn-husk dolls in the store window as an advertisement for the bazaar. But Amanda was empty-handed. "Do you need more corn husks already?"

"No, there's enough to last all day." Amanda let out a big sigh, her expression crestfallen.

Kaylee had a sinking feeling in the pit of her stomach. "Did something happen?"

Amanda slid Reese a sidelong glance.

Reese gave Kaylee a nod and a small wave. "I have to be going. Good to see you again, Amanda."

Kaylee smiled, appreciative of his thoughtfulness. When he was gone, she suggested, "Why don't we go to the workroom and talk?"

Amanda followed Kaylee upstairs and dropped onto a stool at the table.

Kaylee sat down beside her. "What happened?"

Amanda's eyes filled with tears, but she blinked them back. "Your friends were wonderful and so much fun to work with," she assured her. "Then I left to pick up lunch orders for everybody, but when I got back Sandra Cameron was there."

Kaylee smiled as she pictured the spunky and petite chairwoman of the Island Grove charity foundation. "She's quite a dynamo, isn't she? I've heard she's a terrific fund-raiser. I met her when the Petal Pushers were deciding which charity we wanted to donate to during the fall festival. What was she doing at the lighthouse?"

"She stopped by to see the finished crafts and asked the Petal Pushers to make more for the bazaar than she'd first requested."

"But the Petals are already swamped, aren't they?"

"It's not that. When Jessica introduced me to Sandra, she gave me the coldest once-over and made me feel an inch tall."

Kaylee sighed. She hated to hear that. "I'm sorry she was rude to you. I'm afraid people are going to give you looks until this blows over."

"But that wasn't all. She said I needed to leave, that people on the board of the charitable foundation wouldn't want me working there." Amanda burst into tears. "She acted like I'd have my hands in the till the minute I thought no one was looking."

"Surely she didn't mean that."

Amanda wiped her eyes. "Oddly enough, I sort of understand her position. I saw the article with my picture in the newspaper. The charity doesn't want to be associated with someone like me."

"But you're not a thief."

"They don't know that." She sniffled and put on a determined smile. "I had fun making those dolls. Maybe I could work on them at home. That way no one would know I was involved."

"No, you're not going home." Kaylee gestured to the table, then moved her nearly finished driftwood arrangement to the other end of it. "You can work right here." She squeezed Amanda's shoulders. "I'll deal with all the customers, but I'd welcome your company while I work on the fall festival orders."

"Really?"

"Yes, really." Kaylee thought for a moment. "I'll deliver the dolls you make to the lighthouse myself."

"Please don't say anything to Jessica or DeeDee," Amanda said. "They both stuck up for me—innocent until proven guilty and all that. But Sandra was insistent about keeping up appearances if the Petal Pushers wanted to work with the Island Grove charity in a public place like the lighthouse."

"Don't worry. I won't tell anyone." Kaylee felt sick about the situation, and her heart went out to Amanda. She hoped her friend's name would be cleared soon.

Later, as the afternoon wound down, Andrew made two birthday bouquet deliveries on his way home.

Kaylee stood and stretched her tired back. It ached from leaning over the worktable all afternoon. But she'd finished the all-white arrangement, and it was more striking than she'd expected. It was ideal for the modern art gallery. She was confident that Nora would be delighted with it.

Kaylee assessed Amanda from the corner of her eye. She had been slender to begin with, and Kaylee suspected she'd eaten next to nothing since the robbery.

"I have an idea," Kaylee said. "Why don't you and Madison join me for supper? I made chicken pot pie in the slow cooker this morning. It's served over biscuits. It's my favorite fall supper, and I always make enough for an army."

Amanda finished trimming a corn-husk doll's skirt. "I should say no—you've done so much for us already—but I'm going to take you up on it."

Kaylee grinned. "Good."

"First I need to pick Madison up at Chloe's house. They're making posters for their booth at the bazaar."

"Perfect. That'll give me time to get the biscuits in the oven."

Amanda and Madison arrived at Wildflower Cottage just as Kaylee slid the biscuits out of the oven.

Madison giggled as she played with Bear on the kitchen floor.

Kaylee winked at Bear, who frolicked around the girl, playing tug-of-war and fetch with his usual high spirits.

Amanda set the table while Kaylee piled their plates with buttery biscuits and warm chicken pot pie from the slow cooker. She poured some kibble in a bowl for Bear, and the dog ate hungrily. Then the trio sat down and savored their meal.

After supper as Kaylee stacked the dishes in the sink, she studied the sky out the kitchen window. "We have a little time before dark. Should we take a stroll on the beach?" It was only a short walk to the West Sound public beach area. "I could use the exercise, and I know Bear could too."

"Yes!" Madison hugged Bear. "Can I put him on his leash and walk him?"

"Sure. Just don't let him walk *you* when we get there. He tends to get excited by all the gulls, and he tries to take off with them."

They ambled along in silence, and Kaylee hoped the surrounding beauty was as much a balm to Amanda's soul as it always was to Kaylee's. Inland, the island was home to eagles and foxes, and near the water she spotted seals and caught occasional glimpses of an orca whale breaching the West Sound waters. At the dock, they climbed down the metal steps that led away from the road and down to the beach, making it feel very private.

While Kaylee thought the ocean spray and stiff breeze made it too cold to go barefoot, Madison peeled off her shoes and socks. She and Bear started down the beach with Kaylee and Amanda, but soon girl and dog outdistanced the women.

Bear's excitement made them all laugh as he tugged on his leash, chased the waves coming in and going out, and raced after the seagulls, barking happily the whole time.

"Thank you so much for this." Amanda waved an arm at the sand and the sky. "It's good to hear Madison laughing. That doesn't happen very often at home now."

"It will again, and hopefully it won't be too far in the future. I haven't uncovered anything specific yet, but after talking to Joseph Liddon this morning, it confirmed my feeling that the sheriff was too hasty in arresting you."

Amanda didn't respond, but for several minutes, she kept walking as she stared out over the ocean. Gulls screamed and dived into the water all around them. Finally, Amanda cleared her throat. "I don't think your investigating will be necessary."

Kaylee stopped and faced her. "What do you mean?"

"I hate to admit it, but I think I know who took the jewelry."

Kaylee's mouth fell open, and she felt as if someone had smacked her hard between the shoulder blades. "Who are you talking about?"

Closing her eyes briefly, Amanda's voice was faint when she finally spoke.

"What?" Kaylee leaned close to hear over the sound of the crashing waves.

"I almost said something earlier, but I wasn't absolutely sure. I'm still not." She dug a hole in the sand with the toe of her shoe. "I know how it feels to be unjustly accused, and I don't want an innocent person to get hurt."

Kaylee laid a hand on Amanda's sleeve. "Who are you trying to protect?"

Amanda stared down the beach to where her daughter was running with Bear. "Have you met Madison's friend Chloe yet?"

"I may have seen her around town. I'm not sure. Why?"

"She's in Madison's class, but she's seventeen, two years older than Madison and most of the other sophomores. She's a quiet girl, kind of a loner." Amanda brushed her blonde curls out of her eyes. "From the bits and pieces she's shared with me, she's had a chaotic home life for years. It seems that she has too much freedom, and no one keeps a very close eye on her. She missed so much school that she had to repeat two years. Madison brought her into the jewelry store once. After that, Chloe started coming in by herself after school."

"I don't understand." But she was afraid she did.

They started down the beach again. "I've answered my attorney's questions for hours, including making a list of every person I remembered being in the store in the last two weeks. Chloe stopped in a few times."

"Did she act suspicious?" Kaylee asked.

"Not really. The first time when she came in with Madison, Mr. Liddon was gone. Chloe was enthralled with some necklaces and wanted to try them on. I couldn't see any harm in it. Then when she dropped by alone, she never stayed more than ten or fifteen minutes."

"So, what makes you suspect Chloe stole the jewelry?"

"She was in the store just before closing time on the day the jewelry went missing." Amanda paused as Madison and Bear raced back to them and then kept on going. "I heard that she had a shoplifting record from an incident when she was thirteen or fourteen."

"You've been keeping this to yourself?" Kaylee thought that was extremely unwise. She gazed at the pinkish-orange sunset over the water. "It's wonderful that you want to protect Chloe if she's innocent, but would Madison understand your risking prison to protect someone else?"

Amanda wrapped her arms tightly around herself, as if she were suddenly freezing. "I hope if I keep quiet, the police will find the real thief and Chloe will never have to be questioned. That would be so traumatic for her. Even if she's innocent, she might never get over it."

"When she tried on jewelry that first time, nothing turned up missing?"

"No, but the day of the robbery, Mr. Liddon called me away from the counter to assist him. When I returned, Chloe had already left. It was closing time, so I put things away and didn't think anything of it."

"Would you have noticed if anything was missing?" Kaylee asked.

"I think so, but we were in a hurry and talking as we worked. We don't count each piece every day. It wasn't until Mr. Liddon was putting out the displays the next morning that he realized an emerald necklace was missing. Then we did a full inventory."

"You have to tell Mr. LeMasters about Chloe."

"I know but not yet. The trial is still almost two weeks away. If nothing is found within a week, I'll talk to Chloe myself and ask her to bring the jewelry back or leave it where it can be 'found.'"

"Are you sure it's a good idea to wait?"

Amanda gave her a pleading look. "You need to understand that she's a shy, rather troubled girl, and she needs an adult she can count on in her life. She thinks of me as her friend."

Bear barked close behind them.

Both Kaylee and Amanda jumped.

Kaylee glanced over her shoulder. Madison was half a dozen steps behind them. The sound of the waves had drowned out her approach. How much had she heard?

"Who are you talking about? Who thinks of you as a friend?" Madison asked her mom.

"Chloe."

"True." Madison bent down to pat Bear. "She even told me once that she wished you were her mom."

Kaylee remained silent as she followed Madison, Amanda, and Bear back to Wildflower Cottage.

Was Chloe such a great friend? Not if she was the thief and willing to let Amanda take the rap for it.

7

Tuesday morning at Death by Chocolate, Kaylee waited until Jessica helped the last customer and then pulled her aside. "Got a minute?"

"What's up?" Jessica's makeup didn't quite cover her red nose. "If it's about yesterday, DeeDee and I are so sorry about Sandra Cameron talking to Amanda like that." She grabbed a tissue and sneezed into it twice. "Excuse me. Mrs. Cameron meant well, I suppose, but that was so wrong."

"I agree, but it's not about that." Kaylee tried to ignore the enticing chocolate and coffee aromas filling the bakery. "I wanted to ask you a favor."

"Sure." Jessica rubbed her forehead and winced.

"Are you okay?"

She forced a smile. "I'm fine. Just an awful allergy headache."

Over Jessica's shoulder, Kaylee caught sight of something sparkly. It was a girl's fringed shirt covered in rhinestones. Each time the girl sitting by the window swiped across her phone, the fringe swung and the sequins twinkled. One silver earring in the shape of a lightning bolt hung almost to her shoulder.

"Who's that?" Kaylee whispered.

Jessica glanced over her shoulder. "Chloe Padgett. I think she's a sophomore. I call her my fringe girl."

"Her shirt?"

"Yes, she must have half a dozen shirts and jackets with fringe." Jessica lowered her voice. "And she lurks on the fringe, part of the morning crowd but still alone."

"She's always alone?" Kaylee asked.

"Frequently. She comes in on weekends or after school or—like now—before school. She's rarely with anyone." Jessica sneezed again. "So, what can I do for you?"

"I want to talk to the janitor who cleans after hours for Joseph Liddon. I wonder if he's seen things he never reported."

"You think he's covering for someone?"

"Not exactly," Kaylee answered. "He just might not understand the significance of certain things."

"When did you have in mind?"

"Now, before The Flower Patch opens. Would you come with me?"

Jessica studied the room. "Gretchen has things well in hand, so I can pop out with you to see the janitor, although I'm not sure what help I can be."

"Two pairs of eyes and ears are better than one. See if anything I ask sparks a secretive expression or a flash of anger. And feel free to jump in and ask questions yourself."

"Will do. Lead on, Sherlock."

When they stepped out of the bakery, Kaylee noticed a short, wiry man in a black T-shirt standing on the sidewalk in front of The Velvet Box with a bucket and a squeegee. He was washing the large picture window.

Kaylee gestured to the man. "We're in luck. "Let's go." Glad that Bear was asleep in her office, she crossed the street before she lost her nerve.

Jessica hurried to keep up.

Kaylee approached the man. "Excuse me. Do you also clean inside the store?"

He met her gaze, clearly puzzled. "Yes. Ronald Borton's the name."

Kaylee nodded at Jessica. "This is Jessica Roberts, owner of Death by Chocolate, and I'm Kaylee Bleu. I own the flower shop there." She pointed at her store. "We're friends of Amanda Denman's. Could we ask you some questions?"

"Ask away, but I've only worked here a few months."

"Did you ever talk to Amanda?" Kaylee shifted uncomfortably in the wind. She didn't like standing in front of the store's large window. Hopefully Joseph was back in his office and wouldn't see them.

Ronald's smile helped her relax a little. "Yes, nice woman. Always thanked me for keeping the store clean."

"What time do you work here?"

"It depends. I usually come in at five thirty in the evening and work in this store till eight Monday and Wednesday nights. I clean in other buildings the rest of the week." He held up the squeegee and grinned. "Except for washing windows. It's much easier during daylight hours. Hard to see streaks and smears at night."

Jessica stepped forward. "Do you have a key to the building?"

At her friend's blunt question, Kaylee held her breath, expecting him to refuse to answer.

Ronald scratched his head. "No need to have a key. Mr. Liddon has one. And when he goes home before I'm done cleaning, Thomas Rider locks up. Night security guard. He's worked here for years. Stays on duty all night, keeping an eye on this store and a few others."

Kaylee nodded. Ronald and the night watchman had both had a chance to rob the safe. On the plus side, cleaning staff were almost invisible to the people around them. Being unnoticed, they often saw and heard things.

"Do you ever notice unusual people—customers—hanging around the store?" Kaylee persisted. "People who seem out of place?" *Like Chloe.*

Ronald rubbed his chin. "They get a lot of lookers. You

know, window-shoppers who never buy. But I don't remember anyone in particular."

"I assume the store has a security system in addition to engaging the services of a night watchman," Jessica remarked.

"Yes, it does."

"Wouldn't an alarm go off if someone broke in?" Jessica asked.

Ronald brushed a hand over the top of his head. "We haven't used it for several weeks."

"Why not?" Kaylee chimed in.

"Ever since that big lightning storm last month, the alarm system's been on the blink. It goes off for no reason." He glanced at the store entrance. "I heard that Mr. Liddon started getting charged for emergency services for the false alarms. The firm on the mainland's been here twice to work on it, but it keeps going off when nothing's wrong. I'm betting the whole system will need to be replaced."

Kaylee tried to keep a straight face. She was thrilled that the janitor was so open, but if he worked for her, she'd be furious that he'd admitted to two strangers that their security system was disabled.

"What about security cameras?" Jessica asked.

"Nope. Never had a need before."

Just then the front door opened. Joseph stormed out, his eyes bulging as he glared at Kaylee. "What are you doing here again? Leave right now, and don't come back."

Ronald shuffled his feet. "We were only passing the time of day."

"I'm not paying you to chat out here," Joseph snapped. "I can guess what you're discussing. I don't want you attracting the wrong kind of attention." He made a stiff bow to a couple of curious passersby and disappeared inside the store.

An awkward silence ensued.

Ronald picked up his squeegee. "Anything else?"

Kaylee bit her lower lip, trying to decide how to phrase her last question. "Do you think it's possible that Mr. Liddon jumped the gun in accusing Amanda? After all, he accused her even before that necklace was found in her house."

Ronald pulled himself up to his full height, which was still a couple of inches shorter than Kaylee. "I know he was rude just now, but he's a good boss. He wouldn't make an accusation and let his hired help go to jail unless he was sure."

Kaylee nodded as if in agreement, but she thought Joseph Liddon had acted like anything *but* a good boss. "Thank you for your time."

Jessica waved at him, then led Kaylee around the corner of the jewelry shop.

Kaylee lowered her voice. "While we were talking, it occurred to me that the person who could most easily make off with the jewelry is Joseph himself."

Jessica raised her eyebrows. "What?"

"It's common enough—a store owner stealing from himself, pawning the items, and also collecting on the insurance."

"Maybe, but I've seen those TV shows where people try to pawn stolen goods and get caught. I don't think it's as easy as it used to be." Jessica sneezed and tightened the scarf around her neck. "Anyway, you heard what he said. Joseph is a good boss."

Even if he was, Kaylee knew that severe money problems could make some people act out of character. If only she could get a glimpse of Joseph's ledgers. While she admired the janitor's loyalty, she suspected it was misplaced.

Kaylee turned her back to the wind. She used the note-taking app on her phone to jot down the janitor's comments: the hours he worked, the faulty security system, the routine for locking up. Then she faced her friend. "What were your impressions?"

Jessica pulled her coat collar up around her ears. "I thought Joseph overreacted to seeing us. Yes, he's under stress, but he acted like he was afraid of us talking to his employee."

"I thought so too."

Jessica blew her nose. "I like Ronald, but I suspect either his loyalty or his fear of losing his job will keep him from telling you anything helpful about Joseph Liddon."

"I agree," Kaylee said. "Thanks for coming with me."

"I really should get back to work unless you still need me for something."

"No, I can take it from here."

Jessica eyed Kaylee suspiciously. "Take what from here?"

"I'm going to check the back door. Their security sounds iffy at best."

"But what can you learn in broad daylight? Their alarm wouldn't be set even if it was working right now."

Kaylee explained about her sticking doors in The Flower Patch and how Reese told her that most everybody had swollen doors and windows.

"I deal with that problem too."

"Sometimes swollen doors don't latch properly, right?" Kaylee continued. "Someone could close a door, thinking it automatically locked, but the swollen frame kept it from latching. That could happen by accident—or on purpose."

Jessica whistled. "You mean so the night watchman could come back later and give the sticking door a good shove and get in?"

"The night watchman *or* the janitor. Or anyone else who works there."

"I'll come with you when you check the alley."

"Okay. I'll be quick. Then I have to get to work too."

Together they started down the gravel drive of the alley. After standing in the cold wind, Kaylee welcomed the relative calm behind the building. Only three cars were parked in back near a large, green trash receptacle probably used by all the stores. Each shop had its own fire escape leading to the second floor.

Voices drifted into the alley from somewhere.

"Listen." Jessica poked Kaylee in the ribs and pointed to a small window above the jewelry store. It was open a few inches. The voice coming from the room belonged to Joseph.

Jessica gestured to the fire escape underneath the window. She pantomimed climbing up to the tiny platform above to listen beside the window.

Kaylee shook her head vigorously.

But Jessica ignored her and crossed the drive in three strides. Then, step by cautious step, she crept up the half-rusted metal fire escape.

Though Kaylee motioned frantically for Jessica to come back down, she debated joining her friend.

The voices were even louder by the time Jessica crouched at the top of the landing.

Shaking her head again, Kaylee followed and quietly inched halfway up the fire escape. The conversation was much clearer there. Since Joseph's office was on the first floor, what was this room? An apartment? Storage? She listened hard.

"If that's all, I'll finish my report and head home to bed. It's been a long night." A chair scraped the floor inside the room.

"Thanks, Thomas." Joseph sounded less pompous and more worn-out. "I've let business worry me too much. It's always slow once the summer tourists go home. It isn't the locals who buy most of the merchandise."

"No sir." The man's voice moved away from the window, and Kaylee strained to hear. "If you need anything else, just say the word."

"I appreciate your help," Joseph said. "You'll find a little extra in your paycheck this week."

Oh, how she wished she'd taped that conversation. If business was bad, why would Joseph be giving a bonus to the security guard? Was it a payoff? And what kind of "help" had he provided that merited a reward?

Her mind spun in several directions. Maybe Thomas had removed the jewelry during the night at a time when Joseph had a solid alibi. When it was pawned, they could split the money. Then Joseph could collect once more by filing an insurance claim.

Kaylee reached up and tapped Jessica's leg to signal her to leave.

Her friend shook her head while pinching her nose.

Kaylee stared in horror at Jessica's flushed face. Was she about to sneeze?

Inside the room, a door opened and slammed shut, and a different voice burst out, "Why did you do it? I have a right to know!"

Jessica leaned closer to the window, ignoring Kaylee's desperate tugging on her jeans leg.

The strident voice went up a notch. "I mean it. You didn't even warn me!"

"Keep your voice down," Joseph cautioned. "There are customers in the store."

"That's your problem. You can't do this to me!"

Jessica gasped, then clamped a hand over her mouth.

"Did you hear that?" Joseph asked. "It sounded like it came from outside."

Kaylee flinched as the store owner's angry face appeared at the window. She grabbed the handrail to flee down the fire escape.

"Hey!" Joseph shouted.

Out of the corner of her eye, Kaylee saw Joseph's arm shoot out the window, hand stretching toward Jessica.

She jumped back out of his reach. As if in slow motion, Jessica's foot slipped on the fire escape. She grabbed for the railing, but her hand clutched empty air. She plummeted backward and landed in the alley below with a hollow thud.

8

Kaylee clattered down the remaining fire escape steps and raced to Jessica. "Are you all right?"

Jessica groaned and opened her eyes. "Wind knocked out of me," she gasped. "My leg hurts."

"Don't move." Kaylee pulled off her jacket, rolled it into a pillow, and positioned it under Jessica's head. Glancing up at the open window where Joseph hung out, she shouted, "Call an ambulance! She may have a broken leg." *Or back.*

"You were trespassing. I won't file a complaint, but I'm not liable either."

"Just call an ambulance!" Kaylee shuddered as she gently lifted Jessica's pant leg, horrified at how swollen her ankle already was.

Joseph disappeared, and Kaylee heard him on the phone calling 911.

Shivering in the morning chill, Kaylee gripped Jessica's hand. "You'll be all right."

Jessica tried to smile. "So much for Sherlock and Watson."

"Yes, I'd say our cover is pretty much blown."

"But I saw something," Jessica whispered, her eyes like black coals in her ashen face. "I saw something!"

When she took a late lunch that day, Kaylee and Bear dropped by Jessica's house to check on her. While she'd been immensely relieved when the X-rays showed her friend hadn't broken her ankle, it had still been badly sprained.

Kaylee rang the doorbell as Bear danced around her feet. The dachshund had been here before, and he was obviously excited about another visit.

Jessica's husband, Luke, answered the door. "Are you here to see the patient?" he asked by way of greeting.

"Yes, and I hope you're keeping her in line," Kaylee said.

He chuckled. "I'm trying."

"I'm in here!" Jessica called out.

Luke went into the kitchen while Kaylee let Bear scurry into the living room ahead of her.

Jessica lounged in a leather recliner, her raised ankle supported by a thick pillow. On a snack tray beside her was a cup of tea, a couple of books, a TV remote, and a large box of tissues.

Bear sat next to Jessica's chair and peered up at her.

"How are you feeling?" Kaylee asked.

Before she could answer, Jessica sneezed once, then three more times in rapid succession.

"Bless you." Kaylee pulled a chair closer.

Jessica grabbed another tissue, wiped her eyes, and blew her nose, then tossed the tissue into the small wastebasket by her chair. "Honestly, these allergies are almost worse than the sprained ankle." She smiled wryly. "I'm sorry about creating a scene at the jewelry store. Some detective I turned out to be."

"I'm just relieved that your ankle isn't broken."

"Well, if it had been, it would have been my own fault. You tried to stop me from climbing up there."

Kaylee couldn't help but feel responsible. "You aren't going to work this afternoon, are you?"

"No, the swelling is too bad, and I'm supposed to keep it

elevated for a couple days. Plus, I'm sore all over. Gretchen is going to keep the place running while I rest up."

"Is there anything I can do for you at the bakery? Remember I'm right next door."

"I know, but you've already got your hands full with Mary gone, not to mention trying to help Amanda. I called DeeDee, and she's dropping off some flint corn and wire wreaths so I can use my time productively. I'll work on the crafts for the bazaar while I watch movies."

"It sounds like you have everything under control." Kaylee hesitated. "Could we talk about the incident in the alley? Tell me what you could hear when you were right by the window."

"Let's see." Jessica straightened in her chair and readjusted her pillows. "Joseph was talking to someone named Thomas at first."

"Yes, that was Thomas Rider, the night security guard." Kaylee made a note in her phone. "But then he left—"

"And someone else burst in, somebody really angry. I heard him accuse Joseph of something shady."

"And then you fell to the ground. While we were waiting for the ambulance, do you remember saying that you'd seen something?"

"I did? My recollection of those last five minutes is pretty hazy."

"I'm pretty sure that's what you said. What was it?"

"I don't know." Brow furrowed, Jessica leaned back and stared at the ceiling.

Kaylee pressed her lips together to force herself into silence. *Come on, Jess. Think.*

"I know!" Jessica leaned forward eagerly. "I was crouched close to the open window when Joseph popped his head out and startled me. Just before I jerked back and fell, I caught a glimpse of someone right behind him. I don't know who it was, but it was a young man."

Kaylee frowned. "A teenager?"

Jessica sneezed again. "Sorry. He could have been a teenager. He was dressed like one, but he might have been in his early twenties."

"I don't know anyone connected to The Velvet Box who fits that description, do you?" Kaylee asked. "I need to find out who it was and talk to him. Or at least report his name to the sheriff or Amanda's lawyer."

"If memory serves me right," Jessica said, reaching for a tissue, "the Liddons have a son who could be about that age. He must have graduated from high school four or five years ago."

"Really? Do you remember his first name?"

"Jon or Jason or Jackson—one of those *J* names."

Kaylee made another note. "Would the school have back copies of yearbooks?"

"Probably. But I know an easier way to find out. The public library's reference section has old yearbooks. Just go back four or five years."

"Great. I'll do that."

"If that young man was Joseph's son," Jessica continued, "what do you suppose he was accusing his dad of doing?"

"I don't know. What if the jewelry store is in trouble? Joseph said something to Thomas about business being slow, didn't he?"

"Yes, he said the tourists were gone and the islanders didn't buy much."

"Let's assume that Joseph is in financial trouble. Maybe the young man—his son—heard his dad's business wasn't doing so hot. If he's an only child, the store is probably his inheritance. Maybe he tried to borrow money from his dear old dad, but Joseph finally put his foot down. So maybe the son comes home to demand some money. And maybe he reads the article in the newspaper and suspects his dad stole the jewelry for insurance purposes. He sees his inheritance going down the drain, and he's angry."

Jessica raised one eyebrow. "That's a lot of maybes."

"Well, okay, then how about this? The son realizes his dad is in financial trouble when he gets turned down for a loan, and he comes back to town without telling his parents and takes the jewelry himself. He could know the combination to the safe. Or know where the keys to the glass cases are kept."

Jessica thought for a moment and nodded slowly. "It makes sense."

Kaylee tapped out a note on her phone, then dropped it into her purse. "I'd better get moving, but this has been a real help." She stood. "Is there anything I can do for you before I leave?"

"No thanks. Just promise to keep me in the loop while I'm laid up."

Kaylee nodded. "And if I find young Liddon's picture in a yearbook, I'll send you a photo to see if you recognize him as the young man you caught a glimpse of. Come on, Bear."

On the way to The Flower Patch, Kaylee swung by Amanda's cottage to see if she wanted to work on crafts at the shop again. She could stay safely out of sight upstairs in the workroom. Kaylee felt strongly that stewing at home couldn't be good for her friend's emotional health.

When Amanda answered the door, she smiled, but it was glaringly obvious that she'd been crying.

Kaylee gave her a hug. "Are you all right?"

"I'm fine." Amanda led her and Bear to the kitchen. "Can I get you some coffee?"

"No thanks. I can't stay." She noticed the crumpled tissues by Amanda's coffee cup. "A weepy day?"

Amanda produced a wan smile. "I hold it together well until I drop Madison off at school. Then it washes over me that I'm a single mom who may well be headed to jail."

"Is Mr. LeMasters giving you that impression?"

"No, but I've heard the lawyer is 100 percent positive that you'll go free right up to when the jury hands in a guilty verdict." Amanda shook her head. "At least that's how it is in the movies." She brightened briefly. "Did you know Sylvia and Penelope offered to become legal guardians for Madison if I go to prison? I told them she would live with my mother, but wasn't that the sweetest offer?"

"They're wonderful ladies," Kaylee agreed. "I have some news for you." She filled Amanda in on her talk with Ronald Borton and what had happened in the alley.

Amanda gasped. "Jessica was injured trying to help me? That's awful!"

"It's not your fault, and she'll be fine in a few days. She's not letting it get her down. Meanwhile, I'll try to find the Liddon son's picture in an old yearbook, and if it was him, we'll tell Mr. LeMasters."

Amanda snapped her fingers. "You won't need to hunt up an actual yearbook. I've seen Madison researching graduation photos on some website for a school project."

"What's it called?"

"Orcas Yearbook or something like that. I can ask Madison for the address."

"Please do, and let me know right away. Then I can show Jess to see if the boy she glimpsed was Joseph's son."

"You really think it's important?"

"It's just a hunch, but I do think so," Kaylee answered. "I know you don't want to implicate Chloe, but when she's hanging around with Madison, can you let me know if you hear anything helpful?"

Amanda hesitated, then nodded. "Okay."

Kaylee hoped she meant it. "Do you want to work at the flower shop again today? You don't need to deal with customers at all."

"I have to meet with Mr. LeMasters in forty-five minutes. His strategy sessions are long and exhausting."

"If you feel up to it, pop by afterward." Kaylee waved and left with Bear at her heels.

When she returned to the flower shop, she tackled the floral arrangements with the pumpkin vases. Soon all the "vases" were scooped out and treated so they wouldn't rot quickly, and the flowers for the arrangements were trimmed to the proper sizes.

Before she started assembling the bouquets, Kaylee decided to treat herself to a chocolate chip muffin. Maybe she'd get several. Andrew was scheduled to arrive shortly, and hopefully Amanda would come later too.

Leaving Bear behind, she locked the door of the shop and flew down the front steps.

Penelope and Sylvia called out to her from the front of the bakery.

Kaylee laughed. "Are you playing hooky too? I'm heading to the bakery for chocolate." She sniffed in appreciation. "What heavenly aromas waft my way every day."

Penelope smiled sheepishly. "We were there already." She held up her drink. "We just finished decorating the shop for the fall festival weekend and decided we'd earned a reward. I can't believe it's only a few days away."

"If I'm lucky, I'll be ready by the weekend too." Kaylee described the arrangements she'd been making. "Be sure you stop in at Art Attack and see their all-white arrangement. It has twisted white driftwood imported from New Zealand."

"How very artsy. Unlike those." Sylvia pointed overhead at one of the inflatable ornaments hanging from a light pole. "What do you think of the chamber of commerce's Main Street decorations?"

Kaylee chose her words carefully. "Well, they're definitely colorful."

"Yes," Sylvia agreed, "but do you think orange pumpkins and yellow gourds capture the feeling of the island? It seems more like Halloween to me."

Kaylee regarded the nearby stores. "Who do you think will win Best Window Dressing?"

As they discussed the pros and cons of the window displays, Kaylee couldn't help but notice Penelope's silence and her distracted expression. In fact, her attention was focused entirely over Kaylee's shoulder at The Flower Patch. What was she staring at? Kaylee glanced over her shoulder, hoping none of her own festival decorations were askew. But no, The Flower Patch was particularly enchanting, if she did say so herself.

Penelope must have noticed her checking, because she seemed to return her attention to their conversation. But it wasn't long before her concentration wandered again.

"Snap out of it, Penelope," Sylvia barked.

Penelope blinked and stammered, "W-what?"

Sylvia rolled her eyes at Kaylee. "She's hoping to see Andrew."

"No I'm not!" But Penelope's bright blush said otherwise.

Kaylee recalled the day that Penelope met Andrew in her shop and how taken with each other they had seemed. "He hasn't come to work yet," Kaylee stated, hoping her amusement didn't show.

"I wasn't looking for him," Penelope protested. "I don't even know him that well."

Sylvia pursed her lips. "If she doesn't, it's not because he isn't trying. Since we met him, he keeps inventing excuses to see her."

"He does not."

"Just last night, when we got home from work, guess who was waiting on the front porch? That's the second time he's showed up. He'd repotted two of her maidenhair ferns. The first time he visited, he said they were root-bound, so last night he brought two bigger pots and repotted them as a surprise for her."

"For *us*," Penelope clarified. "They aren't *my* ferns on the porch."

"Technically, maybe, but he hasn't spoken five words to me," Sylvia retorted.

Penelope's white curls quivered. "You're making that up. Andrew simply knows a lot about plants, and I'm grateful for his advice. I want those ferns to last for years."

Kaylee listened to this exchange with amusement. *Methinks thou dost protest too much.* Penelope's blushes certainly indicated that she was flattered by Andrew's attention. And if Kaylee didn't know Sylvia better, she would say that she sounded the teeniest bit jealous of the attention her sister was getting.

"Well," Kaylee finally said, "Andrew will be here soon if you want to talk to him."

"Speak of the devil," Sylvia muttered.

Andrew, holding a small white sack, peered into the front window of the gift shop. They all watched as he stared into the store window from several vantage points. Obviously, he was searching for something—or someone. Then he checked his watch and turned away from the window, his shoulders slumping. He glanced up, and when he spotted them, he smiled and waved.

Sylvia snorted, and Penelope's hands fluttered like a small, agitated bird.

Andrew hurried across the street and joined them. "Good day, everyone. I have something for you." He thrust out the white paper bag to Penelope.

"Thank you. What is it?"

"Just a snack. A couple of cinnamon rolls."

"Oh! Well, thank you," Penelope said again. "Sylvia and I will enjoy them."

"Of course." He bowed slightly. "Have a good day, ladies."

Totally distracted from her intention of buying chocolate muffins for Andrew and herself, Kaylee followed him into the flower shop and grinned.

Perhaps Andrew had had enough sweet things for one day.

9

No sooner had Kaylee gathered materials for her first arrangement than a box of miniature flint corn was delivered. This month's Petal Pushers' project was certainly scattered to the four winds. Mary was gone, Jessica was laid up at home, and Kaylee was overwhelmed by work and helping Amanda.

Thankfully DeeDee's life was on an even keel, and she was a whiz at coordinating everything. Kaylee called the bookstore first, but DeeDee wasn't in, so she tried her cell.

DeeDee answered on the second ring.

"A box of flint corn was just delivered, and I have some corn-husk dolls that Amanda made," Kaylee said. "Where do you want them?"

"Perfect timing. I had to pause making the big candleholders when I ran out. Come on by the lighthouse. I'll be here for another hour or so."

Bear was slumbering, so Kaylee left him in the shop. She hauled the heavy box to her car and drove to the lighthouse.

As soon as she parked in the lot, her phone buzzed. She dug deep in her purse. The text was from Amanda. *Found the website that Madison was using: www.MyYearbook.OrcasI.org. Good luck.*

Kaylee hoisted the box to her hip, grabbed her purse, and headed inside. "Here are the corn-husk dolls and flint corn. Where should I put them?"

DeeDee pointed to a table in the corner but said nothing as Kaylee set the box down.

A moment later, DeeDee announced, "There's something I need to get off my chest."

Surprised at her serious tone, Kaylee went to sit by her. "Are you all right?"

"Yes, but I feel bad about yesterday when Amanda came to work here with us. I know I didn't exactly extend a warm welcome. I'm sure you noticed."

"I did. What was wrong?"

"I knew Sandra planned to stop by sometime in the morning, and I wasn't too sure how she'd react to Amanda being here. I believe Amanda, and I really want to support her. But I know Sandra, and I was afraid of her reaction." DeeDee pressed her lips together. "As it happens, I was right to worry."

"What happened exactly? Amanda didn't give me many details."

"When Sandra came into the lighthouse, she said we couldn't afford to have Amanda associated with the projects, that we couldn't take the chance that her reputation might make people avoid our booth." DeeDee sighed. "And with Amanda being charged with robbery, Sandra didn't want her around the money we'd take in after selling."

Kaylee shook her head. "I don't agree with her. I'm sure that most islanders adhere to the innocent-until-proven-guilty theory. But Sandra's the chairwoman of the charity foundation, so her word has to be final."

"I'm just sorry that it happened," DeeDee repeated, "and especially sorry that Amanda heard it."

Kaylee nodded. "Hopefully this will all be over soon. They have to figure out she's innocent sometime." She changed the subject, and they chatted briefly about pricing the crafts they'd made.

"I love the candles with the flint corn standing up around the glass base," Kaylee remarked. "If you like making them, I'll be glad to stock them every fall. I think the tourists would snap them up."

"Really? Some days I wish I could make crafts all day. But I love working at the bookstore too and also making my soaps."

"And spending time with those adorable girls of yours." Kaylee always enjoyed it when DeeDee brought Polly, age eight, and Zoe, age eleven, into The Flower Patch. "Speaking of your soaps, I ran out of your lavender soap, and I have only two more goat milk soap baskets left."

"I'll add that to my growing to-do list." DeeDee made a note in her pocket calendar.

Kaylee didn't know how DeeDee handled everything—running a store, creating her soaps, being a fully committed wife and mother. Kaylee didn't think there was a calendar in the world that could help her juggle all of that.

Then something occurred to her. "Since you've lived here longer than I have, maybe you could fill me in on some local gossip."

"I can certainly try."

"I understand that Joseph Liddon has a grown son."

"Oh yes. Jay Liddon."

"You have a sharp memory."

"Not really. Jay Liddon had quite a reputation in high school." DeeDee paused. "That must have been five years ago by now."

"What kind of reputation?"

"Fast cars, breaking curfew, one or two DUI tickets that somehow mysteriously got hushed up—that kind of thing."

"Was he ever in bigger trouble?" Kaylee said. "I mean, bigger than high school hijinks."

DeeDee nodded. "I believe it was after someone's graduation party. A few kids decided to go outside the city limits and drag race. Jay always had a new car, courtesy of Joseph. There was an accident, and some girl was seriously hurt. I don't recall her name."

"A passenger?" Kaylee asked.

"No, a bystander. You know how twisty the roads are in the

country. There's no visibility around the next curve. Jay sideswiped a car parked by the road—it had a flat tire or something—and the girl standing by the car got hit."

"I don't suppose Joseph Liddon could hush that up."

"No, but I believe it was settled out of court. He paid the girl's medical bills and some other compensation."

Kaylee pulled up Amanda's text message and searched for the yearbook website. After a few taps, a picture popped up. She showed DeeDee her phone. "Is this Jay Liddon?"

"Yes, that's him."

Kaylee studied the photo. "I'm pretty sure I've never seen him before."

"He doesn't come back to Orcas Island much," DeeDee said. "The Liddons shipped him to a distant college after graduation with a good deal of relief, I expect."

Kaylee sent Jay's photo to Jessica, along with her question: *Is this who you saw in Joseph's upstairs window?* Putting her phone away, she asked, "Do you recall what college Jay went to?"

"No, but it was no doubt expensive. Only the best for Jay Liddon. He got a new Mustang convertible for his sixteenth birthday, if that tells you anything."

Kaylee raised her eyebrows.

"Anyway, if memory serves—and I could be wrong about this—I think Jay either dropped out of college or got kicked out. He didn't move home, though."

"Maybe his parents foot his bills wherever he is to ensure he *doesn't* move back home," Kaylee ventured. Could his son's expenses be part of the reason why Joseph Liddon was in financial trouble? Had he been forced to stop giving his son monetary handouts?

Her phone buzzed. Kaylee read the text from Jessica aloud. "'It could be him, but I don't know. The face I saw was more rounded, and the hair was longer and wilder.'"

DeeDee shrugged. "That wouldn't be surprising. Most kids put on weight in college, and I'm sure some grow their hair longer."

Kaylee tapped her fingernail against her phone, thinking about her earlier conversation with Jessica. It seemed more and more possible that Joseph's son could be the real thief. Kaylee's theory was that the spoiled son stole the jewelry—probably to pawn—because his dad wouldn't give him more money to continue the lifestyle he'd grown up with. While DeeDee's information didn't actually support Kaylee's guess, nothing she revealed contradicted her theory either.

If only she knew when Jay had last visited Orcas Island—and if he was actually in town right now. But how could she find out?

"I need to get back." Kaylee grabbed her purse and slung it over her shoulder. "Thanks for the local gossip."

DeeDee smiled. "My pleasure. And I'll get you that soap soon. It's already made. I just need to finish packaging and pricing. I'll have you well supplied before Friday."

"Thank you. See you later."

On the way back to the shop, Kaylee took what her grandpa had always called the scenic route and drove past Joseph's spacious and beautiful brick home. With any luck, she might spot a fast sports car with an out-of-state license plate parked in the driveway.

But the driveway was empty, and the front curtains were shut. Driving by, she studied the three-car garage on the north side of the house. It was large enough to accommodate cars for Joseph, his wife, and a visiting wayward son. What she wouldn't give for X-ray vision right now.

Feeling no wiser than before, Kaylee returned to The Flower Patch. Up from his nap, Bear gave Kaylee a pout when he met her at the front door, as if accusing her of abandoning him.

Kaylee tried to push her ruminations about Jay Liddon

away and focus on the task at hand. This particular arrangement was for High Tide Outfitters, the store on Main Street that rented and sold sports equipment. The order included six corn-husk luminaries to light the sidewalk out front. The huge arrangement for inside the store was to include miniature canoes, tents, bicycles, kayaks, and sailboats, surrounded by *Centaurea cyanus*.

She wouldn't have necessarily chosen cornflowers personally, but owner Vince Mack had been very specific. "They're my wife's favorite," he'd explained, with such a sweet expression that Kaylee hadn't even considered trying to talk him out of it.

"What should I do next?" Andrew asked.

Kaylee startled, then shook her head in embarrassment. "I'm sorry. What did you say?"

Andrew smiled. "You were a million miles away."

"I'm not much of a talker today, am I?"

"We all have days like that," Andrew replied kindly. "I just asked what you want me to do next."

"Let's see. Would you water the Christmas cactus and red poinsettias I'm growing upstairs, the ones that won't be big enough to sell till the holidays?"

"I'd be glad to."

Kaylee held the corn husks tight around the base of a luminary candleholder. "How late can you stay? I think Madison and maybe her friend are coming after school to repot more of their carnivorous plants. If you don't mind, I might have you oversee them." She grinned. "I promise they'll talk more."

Andrew smiled. "Of course. Should I mix more soil for them?"

"I don't think so. I mixed a huge container earlier."

"All right." Andrew went off to water her *Schlumbergera russelliana* and *Euphorbia pulcherrima* as requested. They should be thriving in time for the holidays.

She'd been working only ten minutes when the phone rang. "The Flower Patch. How can I help you?"

"Kaylee, it's Kathy Fitz."

Kathy was the head librarian at the Orcas Island Library, and the community was fortunate to have her. Not only was she friendly and proficient, but she had upgraded the library's computers and implemented several popular programs.

"How are things at the library?" Kaylee asked.

"A tad chaotic at the moment. Do you have time for me to run some ideas past you?"

"Sure." She reached for a pen and a notepad. "What do you need?"

"Long story short, libraries across the state are all required to have a fund-raiser just before Thanksgiving. I'm racking my brain for ideas that won't repeat any of the fall festival activities."

Kaylee tapped her pen on the notepad. "And you want some flower arrangements for it?"

"Yes," Kathy said slowly, "but also decorations that reflect the first Thanksgiving, combining book themes with Pilgrims and Native Americans."

"I'm guessing you're raising money to buy books."

"Right. With so much of our budget going for computer repairs and software, our book fund is sadly depleted."

"What about Between the Lines? Will you do any tie-ins with the bookstore?"

"I hadn't thought of that, but it's a good idea." Kathy's sigh traveled clearly on the phone. "I have no clue what I want. You always design such creative pieces, so I was hoping you could give me some ideas."

"I'll need a bit of time to come up with something," Kaylee admitted. "I can think of obvious connections, like cornucopias and flowers and gourds at the first Thanksgiving. And maybe

I could create a historically accurate Pilgrim garden using real flowers and vegetables they would have planted back then." She scribbled more notes. "I won't be able to get back to you until after the fall festival is over. Probably in a week or so."

"No problem. I feel better knowing you're on top of it."

She had just hung up when the front door of the shop burst open.

"Kaylee?" Madison called.

Kaylee ripped the piece of paper out of the notepad and shoved it into her jeans pocket, then hurried downstairs. "I wasn't expecting you yet."

"We had early dismissal today." Madison gestured to the girl beside her. "This is Chloe."

Kaylee nodded and smiled, recognizing the girl immediately from Death by Chocolate. "Hi, Chloe." The sequined shirt had been replaced by a Western one, also with swinging fringe. What a contrast to Madison's blue plaid shirt and jeans.

Bear trotted over to the girls, wagging his tail.

Madison dropped to her knees. "Hey, Bear! Remember me?"

Kaylee squatted beside her. "Bear's hoping for another walk on the beach with you. You let him explore more nooks and crannies than I do."

Madison grinned. "I'd love to take him out there again."

Chloe hung back, a longing to join in obviously fighting the longing to turn tail and run. Kaylee remembered that feeling as a teen.

Madison motioned to her friend. "Come on. The workroom's up here."

Kaylee followed them upstairs, grateful that she was no longer a teen. While there had been some enjoyable aspects of high school, she found it much easier to be herself now. It wasn't that she no longer cared what people thought of her.

She just rarely let other people's opinions dictate her feelings or decisions.

The girls dumped their books and purses on the worktable next to Kaylee's partly finished luminaries. When she worked alone, the workroom table felt huge. But it seemed to shrink drastically with the addition of two teenage girls. As they rushed off to get their carnivorous plants and soil for repotting, Kaylee scooped up their possessions to stack on the desk in her office.

As she set the books on the desk, one slid to the hardwood floor. Papers tucked into its pages fluttered out. Hoping they hadn't marked anything special, Kaylee picked them up and started to stick them back into the book when a brightly colored piece of paper caught her eye.

It was a flyer announcing a field trip to the mainland to see *The Importance of Being Earnest.* The students in Madison and Chloe's class were instructed to meet on the front steps at school, where they would board a bus that would take them to the ferry.

Kaylee would have to ask them how they'd enjoyed the play. It was one of Kaylee's own favorites. She glanced at the date of the play and inhaled sharply. She checked the wall calendar to make sure.

Yes, the play had taken place the day of the robbery.

And Kaylee distinctly remembered Amanda saying that she had to pick Madison up at the ferry right after work and Chloe had been in the jewelry store just before closing time. If Chloe's entire class had traveled to the mainland, why hadn't she gone? Musing, she wandered back to the workroom.

Soon the girls were back, carrying cups and potting soil, with Bear trailing them.

Andrew set down a large terra-cotta planter of cobra lilies, and they were soon chatting and repotting. Andrew worked quietly alongside them and didn't appear to mind that the girls did much more chatting than repotting. Kaylee loved that Madison sounded so lighthearted.

Still, Kaylee had a question she wanted answered, and she bided her time until there was a lull in the conversation.

"We're nearly out of potting soil," Chloe said. "Is there any more?"

"Really?" Kaylee asked. "I thought I had mixed plenty of soil."

"I'll go mix some more," Andrew offered. He grabbed the plastic bucket and left the room.

While he was gone, Kaylee sat on a tall stool and stretched her tired back. "So how did you girls enjoy *The Importance of Being Earnest*?"

Chloe stared at Kaylee, then squatted down to pet Bear.

Madison's eyes lit up. "I loved it. Did Mom tell you I went?"

"No. When I moved your stuff over to the desk, I dropped one of your books and a flyer for the play fell out."

Whose book had it fallen out of? Had Chloe taken the flyer because it was evidence? Is that why she'd ducked out of sight just now rather than answering Kaylee's question?

"My favorite part," Kaylee said, "is when Gwendolen and Cecily have tea, and they argue over which of them is Ernest's real fiancée. What parts did you two like the best?"

Madison rested her elbows on the worktable. "I loved the scene right after that when Jack and Algernon are exposed. Gwendolen and Cecily realize that neither one is named Ernest and that they're not the people who they claim to be."

"What about you, Chloe?" Kaylee peered underneath the table. *Are you also someone other than you claim to be?*

When Chloe didn't answer, Madison said, "It was too bad, but Chloe didn't end up going."

"Oh no," Kaylee said. "Really?"

"Yeah. I called her when she didn't show up at the ferry,

but she didn't answer. I was worried, but the ferry doesn't wait for anyone."

"When I first moved here, I missed it a few times myself." Kaylee leaned around the edge of the table. "What happened so you couldn't go?"

Up close, Chloe's blush was visible even through her makeup. "I was sick." She leaned over to pet Bear, letting her hair fall over her face.

"That's a shame," Kaylee said. "I hope you get to see the play another time." But it didn't seem like Chloe had been sick. Amanda had distinctly remembered Chloe being in the jewelry store until right before closing time.

An hour later, after Amanda picked up the girls, Kaylee was silent as she swept up spilled potting soil.

"Are you all right?" Andrew asked.

Kaylee nodded. "I'm planning what needs to be done tomorrow. Thanks for helping Madison and Chloe."

After she was alone in the shop, Kaylee locked the front door and went upstairs to do a bit of office work. Bear trotted on her heels. Kaylee wished she could believe that Bear climbed the stairs because he craved her company, but she knew it had more to do with the doggy treats in the filing cabinet.

After Kaylee gave him a treat, she considered what she'd discovered about Chloe that afternoon, examining it from all sides.

"To be fair, it's possible that Chloe felt better later," she told Bear, "and she just wanted to get out of the house. So she went to visit Amanda."

Bear cocked his head as if to say, "But you don't believe that, do you?"

10

When leaving the flower shop that day, Kaylee paused beside her car after Bear jumped in. She studied The Velvet Box, thinking about the stories she'd heard about Jay Liddon. Had he stolen the jewelry when his father refused to give him any more bailouts?

Kaylee climbed into her car and buckled herself in, but she didn't turn the key. Resting her arms on the steering wheel, she ran several possibilities through her mind. What if Jay had discovered the jewelry business was in trouble? How could he have found out? Who might have given him that information? Obviously, his dad hadn't told him.

Then it hit her. How did townspeople usually learn when a business was in serious trouble? When it was put up for sale.

She pulled out of her parking spot and headed to Orcas Island Realty on Sea Cliff Avenue. Douglas Miller was a mainland broker, and he was in his small real estate office in Turtle Cove only two or three days a week. If luck was with her, today was one of those days.

It was, and she parked right in front. The huge plate glass window and overhead fluorescent lights reminded Kaylee of a fish bowl, complete with fake underwater sword plants and java ferns inside. Color photos of properties were stuck to the glass at eye level to catch a passerby's attention.

Kaylee rolled down the window a little and gave Bear a pat. "I won't be long." She'd never have left him if it was summer, but with the cool breezes of autumn, she knew he'd be fine alone for a bit.

He gave her a wounded expression, clearly disagreeing.

When Kaylee walked through the glass door, a man was tidying up his desk and shutting down the computer. The real estate agent didn't appear overjoyed to see her arrive at closing time.

"Mr. Miller? I'm Kaylee Bleu. I own The Flower Patch."

"Yes, of course. Please call me Douglas. So, what can I do for you?"

"I'm located near The Velvet Box, and I heard a rumor that Joseph Liddon was listing it for sale. Is there any truth to that?" she asked, feeling a small pang of guilt for the white lie.

"I can say that Mr. Liddon has not listed his business with me," Douglas said. "But that doesn't mean he hasn't signed with another agent. I can track down the listing for you if there is one." He motioned for her to take a chair. "Who told you about it?"

She thought fast. "It was said in passing in a conversation about something else."

"Let me see." He pressed the power button on his computer to turn it back on. "I'll check the multiple-listing site of all the agents in the area. It may take a few minutes."

"No hurry. And thanks for checking."

Douglas glanced at his watch. "I do have to catch the ferry, though, if I don't want to spend the night in this office."

"Certainly. Where do you live?"

"Shaw Island," he replied without looking up from his computer.

Kaylee nodded and wandered around the small office. On the coffee table were several copies of a real estate magazine. Two photo albums showed property listings divided island by island.

"Nothing on the multiple listing yet," Douglas said. "Let me check one more thing. Maybe your informant misunderstood, and it's Mr. Liddon's house—not his business—that's for sale."

Kaylee nodded, perching on the scratchy brown couch. While flipping through the photo section of homes for sale on Orcas Island, she caught her breath.

A chill passed through her when she recognized a farmhouse. *Payne's Apple Farm!*

She skimmed the listing for the organic apple farm, including a four-bedroom farmhouse, a large shed, acres of fruit-bearing apple trees, garden beds, a pond, a private well, and her favorite building, the barn. This wasn't a traditional barn either. The island barn was specifically designed for the storage of apples prior to shipment to the mainland.

The photo of the barn, with its lower walls made of stone and the upper story red barn wood, instantly transported her back to magical childhood times. Closing her eyes, she could smell the sawdust, the insulation used in the extra-thick walls. The lower story of stone had vents near the floor level that allowed cool air to enter, allowing the warm air to vent above.

Payne's Apple Farm was where she'd often tagged along when Grandpa visited his good friend Ben Payne. After every visit in the fall, Grandpa was sent home with a crate of ripe apples. Grandma made them into apple pies and apple crisps, then canned jars of apple butter and applesauce. In later years, Mr. Payne had hired most of his help, and he'd run the operation from his "office" in one of the sheds.

When Kaylee had visited during the winter holidays, the times at the farm were quieter. The memories were so clear. Kaylee had loved to watch her grandpa and Mr. Payne play board games, cheering Grandpa's colored wooden pegs around the cribbage board shaped like a racetrack. Kaylee always imagined she was watching a miniature horse race.

But *all* her memories weren't heartwarming. She'd also experienced the most intense fear of her life at that farm.

"Nothing on the Liddon house either," Douglas said, startling her back to the present. He shut down the computer again and slid some papers into his briefcase. "I'm sorry, but I have to run."

"No problem. I know what it's like to miss a ferry." She pointed to the photo of the Paynes' farmhouse. "I spent many happy hours at this farm. Mr. Payne was good friends with my grandpa. I was sorry to hear when I moved here that he'd died." She knew from Grandma's letters that Mr. Payne's wife had died nearly five years before that.

"Yes, it's a beautiful farm. Lots of potential." Douglas handed Kaylee one of his business cards, then put on his jacket and hat. "I hope someone buys the farm quickly. There was a break-in there last week."

Kaylee glanced up sharply. The Velvet Box had also been burglarized last week. "Was there much damage?"

"Not a lot. I had the back door of the farmhouse repaired, but I don't have an inventory of the house's contents, so I couldn't tell the police if anything had been stolen or not. I imagine it was a group of kids."

"The owner died a few years ago, so why is the farm being sold now?"

"There was a manager who rented the house and farm from the children who'd inherited it." Douglas held the door open for her, followed her outside, and locked the door. "Now they've decided to sell and split the proceeds."

"That's sad, but it's understandable." Kaylee opened her car door. "Thanks for checking on those properties. I hope you snag a good parking spot on the ferry."

Kaylee was lost in memories of the apple farm on the drive home. In the driveway, she sat in the car daydreaming until Bear nudged her hand to get her attention.

"Sorry, Bear. Come on." While Bear ran to the edge of the yard, Kaylee studied the sky. There were at least forty-five minutes until sundown and another half hour of twilight.

She felt an overwhelming urge to take a walk to Payne's Apple Farm, just like she had so many times with Grandpa. Sadly, it wouldn't carry the name much longer. Kaylee was eager to take one last look around the farm before it had new owners who would undoubtedly make changes.

"Let's take a walk, Bear." Kaylee ducked inside the house and grabbed an old pullover and her heavier parka. She snapped Bear into his plaid woolen coat in case the wind picked up.

When they set off, Bear yanked on his leash, and it required some convincing to coax him to hike in the opposite direction from the beach. Self-indulgent or not, Kaylee wanted to take a trip down memory lane and retrace the steps of Grandpa's morning constitutional.

As they strolled, Kaylee wondered why she didn't walk in this direction more often when there was so much beauty to be seen. Most of Orcas Island was rural and hilly, with curving roads that wound through forests and past artists' studios, fields with old apple barns, and the occasional turn-of-the-century prune-drying barn. It was like going back in time, and Kaylee loved it. Some farmers raised livestock, poultry, or seafood, and the more progressive farms focused on organic foods for the farmers market or local restaurants.

Bear explored the sights and smells in the ditches, as if he were a bloodhound, and Kaylee had to keep tugging on his leash. The wind increased, and she pulled her parka hood up.

Half a twisty mile later, Kaylee rounded a bend in the road to be greeted by the sweet, familiar sight of Payne's Apple Farm.

An Orcas Island Realty sign was stuck in the ground by the driveway. For a wild moment, Kaylee wished she could knock the sign down and buy the apple farm herself.

Bear pulled on the leash, eager to explore, but Kaylee wanted a moment to remember. If she stood in silence, listening to the wind in the trees, she could almost feel Grandpa's big, warm hand wrapped around her small one. She could almost taste the hard cherry candies he kept in his jacket pocket just for her. What she wouldn't give to walk hand in hand with her grandpa one more time.

Sighing, she started up the driveway. With each step, heaviness settled over her, and Kaylee knew why. That visit to the farm had been on an autumn day very much like this one. Only five years old, she'd followed a striped kitten around the farmyard while Grandpa and Mr. Payne visited in the kitchen. The kitten had stayed just beyond her grasping hands, then scampered down a path behind the barn.

Kaylee had followed, trampling the grass that grew around the machinery. She'd searched and called, "Boots! Boots!" over and over, trying to coax the kitten from its hiding place. Then she'd spotted movement in the grass. "I see you, Boots!" she'd cried and taken off running.

She didn't remember exactly where it had happened, but without warning, she'd stepped on something hard and heard a sharp crack. Then the ground beneath her gave way, plunging Kaylee down into the bottom of a dry well.

A thick layer of crunchy leaves had softened her fall, but the rocky sides of the well scratched her arms and legs on the way down.

Kaylee shivered as the memory rushed back at her. She didn't know if the old well had really been twenty feet deep or if it had simply felt like it to a small girl staring up at the tiny opening to the sky.

How she'd screamed and cried and shouted Grandpa's name for what seemed like hours before he found her.

Bear jerked on his leash.

"Sorry, Bear." She reached into her coat pocket for a dog biscuit. "After I walk around the property for a little while, we'll head back." She fed him the treat, tightened the hood of her parka to keep loose hair from blowing across her eyes, and hiked in the direction of the farmhouse.

The long driveway curved around as it descended. What little sunlight was left disappeared as she passed into the shadow of the mountain that rose beyond the apple orchard.

She trekked completely around the house, noting the recently mowed lawn inside the white picket fence and the newly repaired lock on the back door. She hoped the farm sold quickly to a family who would love it as much as the Paynes had.

Kaylee had planned to peek into the windows to see if anything had been left behind, but the house was already shuttered for the winter. After spotting a small gap between the shutters at the kitchen window, she aimed her phone's flashlight into the space but couldn't see anything. She set the phone on the window ledge and tried to open the shutter before she realized how that would look if someone happened to be driving by.

Turning, she surveyed the outbuildings. As long as she was here, she could at least take a peek into the barn.

Kaylee headed farther down the gravel slope toward the barn, wondering how many generations of kittens named Boots had lived at the apple farm since she was a child. Even before she reached the red barn, she noticed a shiny new padlock on the double doors. She sighed. So much for one more sniff of apples and sawdust.

She continued along the circular path past the garage, which was also padlocked, and a little open-sided building that covered the cistern.

"Never wash your hair in anything but rainwater," Mrs. Payne had instructed her, "and your hair will stay soft and shiny."

As Kaylee rounded the circle drive back to the farmhouse, she sucked in her breath sharply.

Instead of being snapped shut, the padlock on the shed where Mr. Payne had kept his office dangled open on a thick chain. Only the heavy wooden bar was in place across the door. After the intruders could no longer get into the house, had they broken in here? *Is someone in there now?*

She forced her feet toward the shed. But Bear stopped suddenly and refused to budge. She dropped his leash and told him to stay.

Lifting the wooden bar on the door, she paused and held her breath. No sound from inside. Slowly she opened the creaky door and peered into the dark shed. Inching forward, she swung her arms in front of her, groping for the thin dangling chain connected to a light bulb overhead.

A gust of wind swung the door almost shut behind her, cutting off the weak October sunlight.

Kaylee dashed back to the door and pushed it open again. She found a paint can and used it to prop the door open. Then she fumbled for the light. Finally grasping the slender chain, she gave it a yank. Nothing happened.

The bulb must be burned out. *Not another one.*

She reached into her back pocket for her phone so she could use the flashlight, but the phone wasn't there. Nor was it in her jacket pockets. Then she remembered setting it on the kitchen window ledge. She'd have to pick it up on her way home.

Sunlight from the door went only a few feet into the shed, but it was enough to see that she was alone. The door to the enclosed corner office was wide open. It was also empty. However, murky shadows wavered under the worktable that ran the length of the shed.

Slowly her eyes grew accustomed to the dim light. She was drawn to one corner under a small boarded-up window. She pushed her parka hood back and crept closer.

Bear barked.

Kaylee glanced over her shoulder and saw Bear standing in the open doorway. "You chicken," she said lovingly. "I'll be out in a minute."

On the workbench she found a one-burner hot plate and a tin coffeepot. Two plates, two stained cups, and a jar of instant coffee were next to it. Were the dishes from the house break-in?

A gust of wind rattled the door against the paint can. Tiny hairs prickled on the back of Kaylee's neck. She checked to make sure the door was still open before moving along the workbench and peering underneath it. Then she brushed the dirt from her knees and the cobwebs from her hair.

A stronger gust of wind shook the shed door and knocked over the paint can. It rolled aside. The door banged shut, plunging the shed into darkness.

A heavy thud jolted Kaylee, and she jumped as the thick wooden bar on the outside dropped into place.

She was trapped.

11

Bear broke into frenzied barking.

Inside the shed, Kaylee stumbled toward the door and beat on it with both fists. She rammed her shoulder against it in hopes of knocking the bar loose. It didn't budge.

Bear continued to bark.

Kaylee kicked the door, and pain shot up her leg. Tears welled up, and she leaned against the door. "Help me!" she screamed.

Even as she yelled, Kaylee knew there was only a remote chance that someone happened to be walking by on the road at this very minute. Even if anyone was out there, her muffled screams would never reach all the way to the road, not over the sound of Bear's barking. On the other hand, maybe someone would stop and investigate why a dog was yelping up a storm at an abandoned farm.

"Keep barking, Bear!" she called.

If only she could send Bear to retrieve her phone. Kaylee collapsed against the locked shed door and slid to the floor as Bear's frenzied barking echoed in her ears.

Lord, please get me out. I can stand anything except being trapped in a dark place again.

Slowly a semblance of peace settled over Kaylee, and she forced herself to organize her thoughts logically. *I'm out in the country and away from any neighbors. The farm is abandoned. There's no point in calling out. It's dark in here. The shed is locked.*

She took a couple of deep breaths and held them, then let them out slowly.

Standing, she ignored the trembling in her legs, then crept

across the shed to the boarded-up window. It was too small for her to wriggle through, even if she could pry off the boards. Breaking down the double doors was out of the question. The wooden bar across the outside was several inches thick.

Gradually Kaylee became aware of a feeble sliver of sunlight illuminating motes of dust in the darkness. She felt her way to a gap where weak light filtered in between two loose boards.

She grabbed the bottom of one board and yanked. It snapped in half, throwing Kaylee backward onto the dirt floor. She scrambled to her feet. After several pulls, she finally broke off the board next to it and lay on her back in front of the hole she'd made.

She squirmed forward through the opening. Her head and right arm were through the hole when she heard a rip. Her left sleeve was caught on a splinter. Hating to do it, she ripped her parka even more in order to push herself all the way through the hole.

Outside, Kaylee knelt in the grass and gulped deep breaths of fresh air.

Bear crashed through the tall weeds behind the shed and nearly knocked her back to the ground in his enthusiasm.

"I'm all right," Kaylee said, untangling his leash from the weeds. Still a bit unsteady, she made her way to the front of the shed. Brushing off her filthy clothes as best she could, she gazed around the farm one last time. Leaves from the madrone trees rustled—a lonely sound.

After retrieving her phone from the window ledge, Kaylee gave Bear another dog biscuit, and they headed back up the road the way they'd come.

A few minutes later she heard a truck approaching around a curve. Pulling Bear close, Kaylee stepped off the road and into the ditch. She'd had enough problems today without getting hit by a truck.

Kaylee could hardly believe her good luck when Reese's familiar black truck drove around the bend. She was simultaneously glad to see her friend and embarrassed for him to see her. Dirty, jacket torn, disheveled, hair probably full of cobwebs . . . Just the picture she'd always hoped to present to him. Maybe in the fading light, he wouldn't notice.

He pulled over to the side of the road and rolled down his window. "What happened to you?"

So much for hoping her disheveled appearance wasn't all that noticeable. "I ran into a bit of trouble on my walk."

"Were you attacked by a bear?" He grinned. "And I don't mean the one on the leash."

Bear yipped in response.

"No, I did this to myself." She explained about her nostalgic trip back to Payne's Apple Farm.

"What was nostalgic about an old shed?"

"Nothing. I noticed the padlock was broken and hanging, and I went to investigate. The wind blew the door shut, and it jammed."

"You'll want to report the broken lock to Douglas Miller, the real estate agent in town." Reese removed his baseball cap, scratched his head, and replaced the cap.

"How did you know it was his listing?"

"A few days ago, he called me to fix the back door of the farmhouse because there'd been a break-in."

Feeling sheepish, Kaylee asked, "Could you do me a favor? When I couldn't get out, I panicked. I hate dark, enclosed places."

"Many people do. Any particular reason?"

She decided to be completely honest with him this time. "I fell in a dry well as a girl, the one behind the apple barn. I was there for a while before my grandfather found me, and it was terrifying. Anyway, I pried off two loose boards on the back of the outbuilding to get out. One snapped off. Could you fix the hole for me and then send me the bill?"

"Sure, if it doesn't have to be done right now. I was on my way to town to finish some built-in shelves for someone's family room. I could swing by the farm tomorrow morning."

Kaylee smiled. "That would be great. Thank you."

"Don't mention it. Can I give you two a lift home?"

"You're going the opposite way."

"It's no problem."

"Thanks for the offer, but Bear and I need the exercise. If we get a move on, we'll be home before dark."

"All right. Enjoy the rest of your walk." Reese glanced over his shoulder and flipped on his turn signal. "I'd better get moving too." He waved and pulled onto the road.

Lost in thought, Kaylee watched him drive away until Bear gave a sharp tug. "You're right, Bear Dog. Time to get home."

On Wednesday morning Kaylee overslept. She didn't have time for a full breakfast, so she grabbed a bagel. "Let's go, Bear!"

The dog trotted over to her and wagged his tail.

She snapped on his leash, then put on his red, white, and blue bow tie. "You're looking very patriotic today."

They dashed out the door and hopped into the car. Amanda was coming to work at The Flower Patch for a few hours. If Kaylee didn't hurry, Amanda wouldn't be able to get in.

Arriving from opposite directions, Kaylee and Amanda met on the sidewalk out front.

"Good morning," Kaylee said. "It sure is a beautiful day."

Bear barked his agreement.

Amanda gazed at The Velvet Box. Then, giving Kaylee a bright smile, she said with determination, "Yes, it *is* a beautiful day." She followed Kaylee up to the porch.

Kaylee wrapped her arm around her friend, mentally kicking herself for her thoughtlessness. "I'm so sorry. I overlooked the fact that you're reminded of your trouble just by coming here. I never meant to make things more difficult for you."

"It's fine. I appreciate having a place to go."

Kaylee glanced across the street and watched a couple leave the jewelry store. "Aren't they stylish?"

They appeared as if they'd just stepped off the pages of a fashion magazine for casual wear. The man had a neatly trimmed black beard, and he wore a blazer, chinos, and a knit shirt. The woman was lovely in her floral midi skirt, cardigan with three-quarter-length sleeves, ankle-strap sandals, and double-strand pearl necklace.

The couple crossed the street and sauntered down the sidewalk in front of The Flower Patch. As the man spoke quietly to his companion, he glanced up at Kaylee and Amanda standing on the porch. Kaylee noticed that his eyes were a startling blue.

After the pair walked away, Kaylee and Amanda sighed in unison, then glanced at each other and burst out laughing.

"Some people have all the luck," Amanda said.

Kaylee unlocked the front door. Inside, she flipped on the shop lights and took Bear off his leash.

The morning flew by. Kaylee divided her time between working on floral arrangements and waiting on customers, and Amanda made more corn-husk dolls.

After Amanda left for a meeting with Mr. LeMasters, Kaylee focused her attention on arranging a bouquet for Kathy Fitz. The library staff was throwing Kathy a surprise birthday party tonight after the library closed. Tina Littlewood, the assistant librarian, had asked Kaylee to arrange a bouquet for Kathy. It was one of Kaylee's most popular arrangements, and it included white Asiatic lilies, yellow roses, and blue delphinium.

Before putting the arrangement together, Kaylee ran to the bookstore. In the gifts section, she was delighted to find a vase in the shape of three colorful books standing side by side. It was perfect.

After school, Madison and Chloe arrived with twenty-five more tiny flytrap and sundew plants.

Bear greeted the girls at the door, and they fussed over him and his little bow tie.

"Where is everybody?" Madison glanced around as she shrugged off her coat.

Kaylee led the way upstairs to the workroom. "Andrew has the afternoon off, and your mom's busy." *Working with her lawyer to try to avoid prison.*

A cloud passed over Madison's face as if she could read Kaylee's mind.

She hurried on. "Did you girls have to carry all those plants on the bus?"

Chloe spread newspapers on the worktable. "Our science teacher gave us a ride."

"Don't worry," Madison added, sounding weary. "We had permission."

As if sensing Madison's mood, Bear curled up at the girl's feet and rested his head on his paws.

"I wasn't worried." Kaylee knew Amanda was aware of all Madison's comings and goings and where she should be at any given time. Kaylee glanced at Chloe, remembering Amanda's comment that no one seemed to keep a very close eye on Chloe. And Chloe *had* been in The Velvet Box the day of the robbery right before closing time. The day her class went on a field trip and she had been supposedly too sick to make it to the ferry.

Everyone set to work. It was quiet in the room while Kaylee began a floral arrangement by filling a pink glass vase with clear marbles and the girls repotted their plants. Kaylee wondered why they weren't talking to each other. She studied Madison discreetly. Something was wrong. Should she pull her aside and ask her about it?

Before she could say anything, the door chimed.

Bear lifted his head and barked.

Kaylee went downstairs as a man in his fifties shuffled into the shop. Everything about him screamed *tourist*—from his gold clip-on sunglasses with the shades flipped up to the binoculars that bounced against his chest. Most likely he was a whale watcher.

She attempted to assist the customer, but the man had no real idea of what he wanted. He gave Kaylee a doubtful expression every time she made a suggestion. So she let him browse as she set out the soap that DeeDee had dropped off earlier. The man eventually left without buying anything.

Kaylee returned to the workroom to finish the floral arrangement. After experimenting a bit, she decided to use white roses, light pink spray roses, and white Alstroemeria lilies.

As she worked, it dawned on her that the girls were still not speaking to each other. Kaylee snuck a furtive glance at Madison. Her downcast expression as she slumped over the worktable spoke volumes. Kaylee tried to figure out the reason for the tension in the room as she arranged the flowers in the vase.

"Why don't you want to help?" Madison suddenly demanded. "You said you would."

"I *will*." Chloe glanced at Kaylee, then away. "I'm helping now, and I'll help set up the booth Friday night."

Kaylee didn't say a word as she trimmed the stems to their proper lengths.

"But this is our project together," Madison insisted. "That includes helping sell plants at the bazaar."

"I said I'd help set up," Chloe snapped.

"There's more to the bazaar than setting up. We're supposed to sell things for two hours. I can't do it all by myself." Chloe's voice was low but distinct. "I don't like waiting on strangers. I don't know what to say."

Madison huffed. "Talking to strangers isn't exactly my favorite thing either."

There was a dead silence, and Kaylee tactfully went downstairs to the cooler for filler plants, choosing both ivy and baby's breath.

Kaylee returned to the workroom and an uneasy truce. Chloe left before the plants were all repotted, so after finishing the get-well arrangement, Kaylee took Chloe's place. Together she and Madison finished the rest of the transplanting.

"You girls have grown an amazing number of plants to sell," Kaylee commented.

"I guess," Madison mumbled. She didn't volunteer anything else.

"I'm betting that you have close to 200 plants for the bazaar," Kaylee continued. "That will raise a lot of money for new lab equipment. Is there a contest for who raises the most money?"

"No."

They worked in silence, filling the wooden trays with the cups.

"I couldn't help overhearing that Chloe isn't going to sell the plants with you during the bazaar," Kaylee ventured. "Were you counting on her?"

"Yes! And she's leaving me high and dry."

"That's certainly not something you'd expect a friend to do."

"She's not really my friend," Madison admitted.

Kaylee raised an eyebrow in surprise.

"I mean, she is my friend sort of, because she's the first

person to be nice to me when I started at this school." Madison took a handful of soil and let it slip slowly through her fingers. "But she's actually kind of weird."

Kaylee remained silent.

Madison drew little circles in the dirt with her finger. "It's mostly Mom's idea that Chloe hangs out with me. She says Chloe needs a friend." When Kaylee didn't answer, Madison finally glanced up. "What?"

Kaylee put an arm around Madison's shoulders, hoping she wasn't about to put her foot in her mouth. "Is there something else wrong too? When you walked in after school, I got the impression you weren't feeling like yourself today." She waited, but Madison didn't answer.

The silence hung on so long that Kaylee regretted asking. She hadn't meant to pry, but something besides Chloe's defection was obviously wrong.

"I shouldn't let it bother me," Madison mumbled.

"Shouldn't let what bother you?"

Madison's shoulders relaxed, and she leaned against Kaylee for a moment. "A stupid kid at lunch." She sighed. "I was eating, and a kid going by stopped and said, 'Hey, look, everybody. It's the thief's kid.' Really loud. Half the lunchroom stopped talking to stare at me."

"Oh, Madison, I'm so sorry." Kaylee ached for her friend's daughter. "You *do* know your mom's innocent, don't you?"

"Of course I do." She sighed again. "But what he said still hurt. And a bunch of kids laughed."

"Your friends?"

"No, probably his friends."

"I imagine you're right. No one who knows you or your mom would believe that." Kaylee pulled her close again and rested her chin on top of Madison's head. As she prayed for wisdom and healing, she felt a teardrop land on her arm. If only she could help this sweet girl.

No matter how inept she felt, Kaylee knew she had to keep trying to clear Amanda's name. The girl in her arms was one enormous reason. And it needed to happen before "the thief's kid" became Madison's permanent brand.

12

Kaylee patted Madison's arm and leaned back. "Do you want to go with me to get the brochures printed? Then I can drop you off at home. I'll call your mom and let her know."

Madison nodded, giving her a small smile. "Thank you for making the brochures." She waved a hand over the long table. "And for the work space and the potting soil you made. I would have used the soil from the garden center and killed them all."

"It's my pleasure. And now you know that these plants actually love soil with few nutrients." Kaylee grabbed her phone and placed a call. "Amanda, is it okay if Madison comes with me to have the brochures printed? I'll bring her home after that."

Amanda sounded hesitant. "Sure."

"What's up?"

"I'm at the attorney's office, and I don't think I'll be home for another hour. But Madison has a house key, and the back door lock has been fixed since someone broke in."

Kaylee tilted her head. Given Madison's disturbing school day, she hated the idea of her brooding at home alone. "After the printing, I need to deliver an arrangement to the library. If Madison comes to the library with me, she'll be home about the same time you are."

"Wonderful," Amanda said. "And thank you."

Kaylee hung up and turned to Madison. "I have to make a delivery to the library too, if you want to check out some books. Anything in particular you like to read?"

"Mostly fantasy. I haven't read much since moving here, and I've missed it."

"Then let's see what they have to whet your appetite again." Kaylee knew the power of a good book when it came to overcoming loneliness or having something to focus on when tempted to worry. "Let's go."

Madison climbed into the front seat of Kaylee's car, and Bear hopped onto her lap. Madison grinned and hugged the little dog, who licked her chin and wagged his tail.

Kaylee was also reminded of the power of a warm, furry friend. *We'll cheer you up in no time, young lady.*

Kaylee placed the birthday arrangement in the back seat, wedging it in with a couple of small pillows, and got behind the wheel.

At the copy store, Madison walked Bear on his leash on the sidewalk out front. Since there were no other customers in the shop, the clerk was able to print the brochures right away. As Madison had decided, they printed seventy-five of the fun facts brochure with lots of pictures and twenty of the other one that contained more scientific information.

While waiting, her phone rang. "Jess, what's up?"

"I just had the most amazing insight." She sneezed, laughed, and sneezed again. "Eight cups of strong coffee in a day make me brilliant."

Kaylee laughed. "Don't keep me in suspense."

"We've been looking at this robbery thing all wrong," Jessica said.

"How exactly?"

"I watched a movie on cable this afternoon—the choices on TV during the day are truly appalling—but it was about a kidnapping."

"A kidnapping? You've lost me." Kaylee glanced out the window at Madison, who was playing with Bear.

"The kidnapping turned out to be a hoax," Jessica responded. "It was a publicity stunt."

"I don't get it."

"There was no kidnapping after all."

Kaylee moved away from the counter and lowered her voice. "Are you saying the robbery might be a hoax?" She couldn't fathom how that could be true.

"Think about it. Joseph admitted that sales were down now that the tourist season is nearly over. And what did he get after reporting the robbery? Tons of free newspaper publicity. I bet he orchestrated the whole thing to drum up more business."

"Well, it's a theory." Kaylee cautioned herself not to throw out the idea just because it sounded far-fetched, as many of Jessica's ideas had seemed in the past. "I'll think about it, but I have to go now."

"Don't forget to tell Amanda's lawyer too," Jessica added.

We'll see. "Talk to you later." Kaylee tucked her phone back into her purse.

After putting the box of brochures in the trunk, Kaylee said to Madison, "We'll take a short detour and drop Bear at home. He needs to run around and get some exercise before dark."

"Too bad," Madison said, scratching under his chin. "But I understand."

After leaving Bear at Wildflower Cottage, they headed for the library. Kaylee never tired of the scenery on the island. Although quiet, Madison appeared to enjoy it too. Kaylee found that being out in nature was a real balm for the soul. And when she couldn't be out in it, driving through it was second best.

"Would you like to see some pictures of my nieces?" Kaylee asked to break the silence.

Madison glanced around. "Sure."

Kaylee pointed to a fat envelope on the console between them. "My parents moved to Florida to be near my brother and his family. My brother, Kyle, and his wife, Linda, live in Sarasota.

Isabella is seven, and Mattie's five. They change so much in such a short time. My mother sends me photos every month or so. It's like watching them grow up right before my eyes."

Madison picked up the envelope and flipped through the pictures. "This is so old-fashioned. Doesn't your mom text or e-mail? She could send you photos faster that way and lots more of them. And short videos too."

Kaylee shrugged. "She does text me, but I still enjoy receiving a letter in the mail. Somehow it feels more personal. I'm apt to read it more than once, but I rarely do that with e-mails. They get lost in my in-box." She shifted gears as she headed up a steep grade. "Plus, I like to put the girls' photos on my fridge. I always intend to print out digital pictures, but I hardly ever get around to it."

At the Orcas Island Library, Madison held the door open while Kaylee carried in the birthday arrangement.

Tina rushed over to them. The assistant librarian's red hair and green eyes were striking with her purple fingernail polish. "The flowers are beautiful." She glanced over her shoulder to where Kathy was helping an elderly couple use a computer. "Let's put them in the back room before Kathy notices." Tina led the way.

As Tina instructed, Kaylee left the flower arrangement on a table that also held birthday cards, a cake, and balloons. She'd try to catch Kathy's attention before they left. On her walk that morning, she'd come up with an intriguing idea for Kathy's Thanksgiving fund-raiser. It would take more planning, but if they started soon, it was doable.

In the meantime, she and Madison headed to the main part of the small library. It housed the fiction and nonfiction collections and a row of computers for public use. The adjoining reading room was filled with tables and comfortable chairs, where patrons read magazines and newspapers from the racks lining the wall.

Madison elbowed Kaylee. "Look who's here."

Kaylee followed her gaze and saw Andrew. He sat reading a newspaper spread out on a table before him.

Madison tiptoed up behind him and said quietly, "Hi, Andrew."

Andrew jumped, saw them, and leaned over his newspaper. "Hello! What are you up to? Still working on your brochures?"

"Kaylee got them printed." Madison grinned. "Now we're all set."

Andrew gave her a high five.

Kaylee nudged Madison gently. "You'd better pick out some books. The library closes soon."

"Okay. See you, Andrew." Madison rushed off.

Kaylee glanced down at the newspaper and was surprised to see it open to the society page. Turtle Cove's consisted mainly of church luncheons, bridal showers, and wedding announcements.

"Anything interesting?" she asked, noticing a photo of Vince Mack, owner of High Tide Outfitters. His family had thrown him a birthday party, and his two sons and all six grandchildren were in the picture. Kaylee smiled. She loved small-town newspapers.

Andrew's bony arms covered half the page. "Nothing much today." He started to fold the paper.

"Wait." Kaylee glimpsed a picture of a smiling couple halfway down the page. Mr. and Mrs. Joseph Liddon were announcing their twenty-fifth wedding anniversary. She leaned closer to read about it, making a mental note of the time and place for their reception. An anniversary celebration was the perfect reason for their son to be in town. Maybe she would be able to meet Jay after all.

Kaylee rested a hand on Andrew's shoulder. "Thanks for covering the Liddon story so Madison wouldn't notice it. She doesn't need to see the man who's ruining her mother's life smiling and announcing a big celebration."

Andrew simply nodded.

She spotted a waving arm out of the corner of her eye. DeeDee stood over by the children's section. Kaylee said goodbye to Andrew and went to join her.

"What brings you here?" DeeDee asked. "Have you finally run through all your grandfather's mysteries?"

"No, I had a delivery to make," she said, lowering her voice, "for a surprise birthday party for Kathy." She nodded toward the young adult section. "I have Amanda's daughter with me. She's searching for fantasy books."

"How's she doing? I can't imagine my girls having to go through her situation."

Kaylee followed DeeDee's glance to where her daughters, Polly and Zoe, were reclining in a couple of purple beanbag chairs, engrossed in their books. "I think Madison's doing as well as anyone could at her age."

"Have there been any new developments since we talked? Did you track down Jay Liddon?"

"No, not yet, but I still think he's a viable possibility. And Jess came up with another of her crazy theories." Kaylee repeated what Jessica had suggested during their phone conversation. "I really can't see Joseph staging the whole thing for publicity, can you?"

DeeDee grinned. "Don't write off her idea just yet."

"You're joking. You really think there's something to it?"

"Jess called me earlier about it, and she mentioned one other very pertinent fact."

"Really? What?"

"She had Luke bring Oliver home to keep her company. Apparently Oliver has been droopy the last two days, but when she talked to him about this new brainstorm, he perked right up."

Oliver was Jessica's prize lavender geranium, which usually sat on the counter at Death by Chocolate. She treated him like a member of the family and predictor of future events. She fretted when Oliver drooped, considering it a bad omen, but when he revived, she claimed it boded well for the future.

Kaylee snorted. "Well, there it is. Case closed."

Kathy's voice sounded over the intercom. "The library closes in fifteen minutes. Please bring your books to the checkout station."

"See you soon. I'd better go nudge Madison along." Kaylee found her with a pile of books stacked on the floor around her. "Time to choose a few and check out."

By the time they'd used the scanner at the self-checking machine, Andrew was gone.

Kaylee and Madison exited the library and got into the car. When Kaylee drove around the curve that followed the harbor, she was startled to see Andrew as she went by. He sat on a bench near the ferry, his coat collar up around his ears. Did he have car trouble? Was he waiting for someone to pick him up?

"We should find out if Andrew needs a ride home," Kaylee said. "Let's go back and ask."

But a couple of minutes later when she swung by again, he was already gone.

"Look." Madison pointed down to the ferry. "Isn't that him?"

Kaylee pulled over to the side of the road and studied the people heading toward the walkway that led onto the ferry.

Sure enough, there was Andrew. Where could he be going so late in the day? Or was he waiting to welcome someone coming to Turtle Cove?

13

After dropping Madison off at home and chatting with Amanda for a few minutes, Kaylee realized she hadn't talked to Kathy Fitz about her fund-raiser. The library was closed and she was enjoying her surprise party, but Kaylee could call her later tonight. She'd taken the call at work and written Kathy's description of the event on her notepad.

She'd drive by the shop for the note—it would only take a minute—and call Kathy when she got home. But when she ran inside the flower shop, she couldn't find the note. What had she done with it? Oh well, it could wait until morning.

Coming back outside, she glanced across the street to The Velvet Box. It was the night they stayed open later than usual. She glanced at her watch and saw that she didn't have much time.

Ronald Borton said he cleaned the jewelry store two nights per week. He'd seemed sympathetic to Amanda's plight and much more willing than Joseph to answer questions. Maybe he could tell her if Jay was currently in town and if he had visited the store in the last ten days.

Since it wasn't quite closing time, Kaylee walked to the alley behind the store. A bright light lit up the entrance. Kaylee grimaced at a new sign on the door: *Keep Out—Employees Only.*

She held her breath and knocked, praying that the janitor answered the door and not Joseph. She didn't relish the idea of being alone in the dim alley with Joseph Liddon.

After a few moments, she knocked again. Pulling her coat more tightly around her, she stiffened her shaky legs. Ever since

Jessica's fall from the fire escape, Kaylee sensed a sinister pall hanging over the jewelry store.

No one answered, and no sounds came from inside. She was embarrassed to admit, even to herself, that she was more relieved than sorry. Letting out the breath she'd been holding, she turned away, glad to hurry back to the safety of her car.

Kaylee hadn't gone three steps before the door opened behind her and Ronald stuck his head out. "Oh, it's you. Miss Bleu, right?"

"Yes." Kaylee glanced at the darkened windows in the room above the store but dropped her voice anyway. "Could I ask you a couple more questions?"

Ronald looked up and down the alley. "I already told you everything I know about what happened."

"You were very helpful, and I appreciate it." She tried to put some warmth into her smile. "So, when something came to my attention, I thought you'd be the man to ask."

Ronald stood a bit taller, but he still appeared wary.

Kaylee glanced over his shoulder into the store's back hall. "Is Mr. Liddon in there?"

"Yes." Ronald reached behind him and softly closed the door. "He'll be busy closing up for another ten or fifteen minutes."

"Okay. I'll be quick. This may sound like an odd question, but I saw an announcement in today's paper about an anniversary celebration the Liddons are having."

Ronald frowned, clearly puzzled. "And?"

Kaylee rushed on, thinking how silly this might sound. "I wondered if perhaps Joseph Liddon's son is back in town for the celebration."

"I don't know their son."

"He's in his twenties, I believe."

Ronald shrugged. "I suppose he could be in town, but I

wouldn't know him even if I saw him. Actually, there's a man in the store right now, but I doubt he's a relative." He pulled an ornate gold pocket watch from his coveralls and opened the lid.

"That's a beautiful watch."

"It was my grandfather's. He gave it to me." He slipped it back into his pocket. "It's five till seven. The young man might still be in the store."

"Thanks." Kaylee's boots crunched against the gravel as she rushed away.

With a faint metallic click, the door behind her closed.

Pausing at the entrance to the darkened alley, Kaylee scanned the street. Several stores were open late tonight to get a jump on the fall festival crowd. She pulled up the collar of her coat, tempted to go home and get cozy. And yet, she didn't dare leave. Jay Liddon—if he was in the store—might hold the key to proving Amanda was innocent.

At the corner of the jewelry store, Kaylee peered around the building. Only a few shoppers strolled down the street. Light from the jewelry store's picture window cast pale orange rectangles on the sidewalk.

The last thing she wanted was for Joseph to spot her, but she had to know if there was a man inside who might be his son. She pressed her back to the brick building.

Two women stared at her as they passed.

Kaylee pasted a smile on her lips and tried to appear casual as she inched closer to the window, stopping short of the yellow patches of light.

Then she held her breath and peeked around the edge of the window. The new clerk stood with her back to the window, showing a tiny white-haired lady a sparkling ring with a diamond so large it looked fake. Joseph was at the cash register keeping an eagle eye on the clerk. With a combination of disappointment and relief, Kaylee saw no sign of a young man.

But as she turned to leave, she spotted a man on the other side of a six-foot-high glass case, examining a crystal sculpture of two bottlenose dolphins. Dressed in a gray suit and a dark gray tie, he seemed to be the consummate thirty-something professional. Besides being older than Jay Liddon, he didn't resemble the picture she'd found on the yearbook site at all.

The man glanced up briefly and, through the glass case, stared through black-framed glasses at the front window. His close-clipped mustache twitched.

Kaylee jerked back and waited for the pounding in her ears and chest to subside. Something about him bothered her. What was it? She edged closer to the window and peered around again. Now the man was talking to Joseph.

Before she could duck out of sight again, Joseph caught a glimpse of her and started for the front door.

Kaylee darted around the corner of the building and raced fifteen steps to the alley entrance, then stepped into the dark, narrow lane. Staying in the shadows, she waited. Nothing happened. She waited some more, afraid that Joseph would check the alley. If he'd recognized her, hopefully he would think she was already back at The Flower Patch.

After a few minutes, her heart stopped its painful thumping. She peered out of the alley onto a quiet street. Joseph was nowhere in sight.

However, suddenly the mustached man in the black-framed glasses appeared, and Kaylee shrank back in the shadows. He crossed the street and strode down the sidewalk in front of The Flower Patch. He kept his gaze straight ahead, not window-shopping or speaking to anyone, and moved like he had a destination in mind. A parked car somewhere? Maybe his ride to the ferry?

Who was he? Something about him nagged her. What was it? She couldn't put her finger on it, but her every instinct said to follow him.

Kaylee slipped out of her hiding place and hustled to the intersection, then crossed the street. The man marched down the sidewalk, zigzagging smoothly between shoppers who poured out onto the sidewalks as stores closed. Kaylee melted into the crowd. It was easy to follow him since he kept moving straight ahead.

When he reached the end of the block, he veered right and, without a backward glance, disappeared down the street. Was his car parked down there?

She sped up.

But then an older man stepped out of a store and bumped into her.

"Pardon me. Didn't mean to plow into you. Oh, hello, Kaylee!" Mr. Billows, one of Kaylee's grandmother's friends, took her arm and guided her out of the way of other pedestrians. "How very good to see you."

"You too, Mr. Billows. I wish I had time—"

"What do you hear from your charming grandmother these days?"

Kaylee groaned inwardly. She couldn't stand and chat or she'd lose her quarry. "My grandma's doing very well." She backed up a step. "She's loving retirement."

Mr. Billows beamed as if Kaylee had said something really clever. "Will she be home for a visit anytime soon?"

"I'm not sure. It's good to see you, but I need to get going now." Smiling and waving, Kaylee rushed to the corner of the store. She peeked around it and sucked in her breath sharply.

The man was gone.

Kaylee pivoted to the right, then the left, confused. She knew he'd gone that way. Even in the side street's murky shadows, Kaylee could see well enough under the streetlights. On the opposite side of the street, a young mother pulled a toddler along behind her and pushed a stroller ahead of her. No one else was in sight.

However, two parking spots stood empty. Had the man been parked there? Had he driven off while Mr. Billows delayed her? Had there been that much time? If only she'd seen the man's car and written down his license plate number. Sheriff Maddox could have identified him that way.

Profoundly disappointed, she turned around to walk back to her car. What a long day. She was ready to go home, eat some vegetable soup, and curl up in front of the fire.

A cat's yowl in the dark alley made her jump, and she glanced over her shoulder.

Then a man reached out of a shadowy doorway, dragging her off the sidewalk.

Kaylee sucked in a deep breath to scream, but the man clamped his gloved hand over her mouth.

The scream died in her throat.

14

Kaylee lashed out with both fists. Twisting from side to side, she struggled to breathe. The gloved hand tightened over her mouth and nose. She was afraid if she fought any longer, the stranger would suffocate her, so she went limp.

The man relaxed his grip. "That's better," a hoarse voice whispered from behind her. "Don't scream. I won't hurt you."

Kaylee nodded with difficulty.

Slowly the man lifted his hand from her face. He paused, his hand still close to her mouth.

When Kaylee remained quiet, the hand dropped.

He gripped her arms and spun her around to face him.

Shaking, Kaylee stared at the dark outline of the man she'd followed. "What do you want?" she demanded, trying to put a steel edge into her voice. Instead, the breathy words held a slight quiver.

"I might ask the same question, don't you think?" the man said. "Weren't you following me?"

Kaylee's heart hammered in the evening's stillness.

"You blew Amanda Denman's best chance to clear her of the theft charges," the man stated.

"What?" Kaylee stumbled backward. His words made no sense. "Why? What are you talking about?"

The man's voice hardened. "I was the only one hunting for the truth about Joseph Liddon. The sheriff certainly isn't."

Kaylee squinted, trying to make out his face in the shadows. Then she dug in her bag and retrieved her phone. She switched on the flashlight and pointed it at him.

She inhaled sharply at the sight of his very light blue eyes. That was what she'd noticed earlier. She flashed back to the investor in the jewelry store who'd said he was interested in buying ruby and emerald necklaces. His eyes had been this color. Then she recalled the man with the beard who had been walking down the street and glanced up at her on the porch with the same stunning blue eyes. "Who *are* you?"

The man reached inside his suit jacket and pulled out a thin wallet. He removed a business card and handed it to her.

Kaylee peered closely and silently read: *Richard O'Connor, O'Connor Investigative Services, Spokane, Washington.* "You're a private investigator?"

"I am. I needed information from the scene of the crime."

Kaylee frowned. There was no information left behind at the jewelry store. The sheriff had taken the only evidence—the emerald necklace found in Amanda's kitchen. "I saw you earlier when you tried to buy gems. You claimed to be an investor."

Mr. O'Connor nodded. "I said I was Michael Scott and I worked for an upmarket retailer. I used that disguise to get into Mr. Liddon's office and check out his books. One of the stolen necklaces was made of rubies. If he'd stolen the jewelry himself, I hoped to tempt him into getting it out of hiding to sell to me."

"Did you learn anything in his office?"

He was silent so long that Kaylee thought he was refusing to answer. "You can trust me," she added. "I only want to help Amanda."

Finally, Mr. O'Connor spoke. "I believe you."

That surprised her. "Why would you? You don't know me."

"I ran a check on you too. And I know where you were when the jewelry went missing."

Kaylee's jaw dropped. *She'd* been under suspicion?

"It's just part of the job." Mr. O'Connor shrugged. "To answer your question, yes, I did learn something from Liddon's books. Thanks to tiny hidden cameras"—he patted the pen in his shirt pocket—"getting photos is fairly easy. One time Liddon went to get some bracelets from his glass cases for me to examine. I snapped photos of his ledgers then. I noted certain large debits and had the police run a check on those dates and where the large amounts went."

"And did you find out anything?"

"The large amounts of money went to his son, and it's happened more frequently lately. It took very little digging to uncover Jay Liddon's rapidly growing gambling debt. If he owes a loan shark, either he or his father could have been desperate enough to steal that jewelry. Or his father could have recently stopped paying the gambling debts, and Jay decided to come home and help himself to the jewelry."

Kaylee nodded slowly. It made sense. It also made her more certain than ever that it had been Jay who'd barged into the second-floor room at the jewelry shop when she and Jessica had been on the fire escape.

She studied his face. "You were wearing a beard at the time, but you were also in the jewelry store with a woman. Beard or no beard, I noticed your eyes. You really should wear colored contacts if you want to go incognito."

Mr. O'Connor smiled ruefully. "Apparently." He peeled off his mustache and wiggled his upper lip. "The lady with me was another investigator from our office."

"Who were you today?"

"Victor Summerlin from a chain of jewelry stores in New York. I claimed that I wanted to buy Mr. Liddon's store to add another outlet to our business." His blue eyes grew icy. "But after Liddon spotted you watching us through the window, he got suspicious and asked for my card. He went back to his office to make a call. No one at the New York outlet had heard of me of course, and he told me to get out."

Kaylee cocked her head. "Who hired you? Mr. LeMasters or the insurance company?"

"The insurance company, although they gave Mr. LeMasters the information about large funds going to his son, probably for gambling debts."

Kaylee wanted to sink to her knees. What had she done? "So, you're employed by an insurance company to investigate this as fraud?"

"I was. Emphasis on *was*."

With a horrible sickening feeling, Kaylee knew he was telling the truth. She had ruined his investigation with her clumsy attempt at playing detective. If only she'd been warned about him. She would have stayed out of his way. Did Amanda know about Richard O'Connor, PI?

"I'm truly sorry. I'd give anything to undo my mistake."

"No need to apologize to me. It's Amanda Denman who deserves an explanation."

Kaylee nodded. He was right. But how could she explain to Amanda that she'd managed to make her precarious situation even worse?

At The Flower Patch Friday afternoon, Kaylee was saddened to learn that Amanda didn't plan to attend the bazaar at the high school that night.

"That's a shame." Kaylee picked her words carefully. "There should be a good turnout for the opening night of the fall festival. Madison's plants should sell like hotcakes."

"I hope so." Amanda packed a box with finished corn-husk dolls for the Petal Pushers booth. "I'll hear all about it when she gets home."

"Wouldn't you rather see her success in person?" Kaylee opened a large, flat box and arranged four flint corn wreaths inside.

"It's the fact that there *will* be lots of people there that made me decide to stay away." Amanda folded the cardboard box shut and taped it. "After the reactions I got from the angry woman who thought I was a disgrace to your shop, plus the chairwoman of the Island Grove charity foundation who didn't want me near any money, I decided not to embarrass Madison tonight by making us conspicuous. What if someone decides to express 'concerns' about me stealing from my daughter's cashbox?"

Kaylee's heart ached for her. "It's true that you might receive some stares since your photo's been in the newspaper, but I think Madison will be disappointed if you don't come."

"Really?" She pinned up a couple of loose curls that had escaped her hair clip. "I only want to help my daughter, not hurt her."

"So you'll go?"

Amanda gave a wry smile. "I'll consider going, but I'm not making any promises."

Kaylee taped her box, set it on the floor, then grabbed a smaller box for the rest of the little corn-husk dolls. Her mind wandered back to her altercation the night before, and she searched for the right words to tell her friend.

Amanda reached across the worktable and touched her arm. "What's the matter? It's *me* in danger of going to jail, not you," she teased.

"That's just it," Kaylee burst out. "I think I actually managed to increase your chances of a prison sentence."

"What?" Amanda sat down hard on a stool. "How?"

With great reluctance, Kaylee told her about the private investigator and how she'd managed to alert Joseph to his presence in the jewelry store. "I had no idea who he was. I was searching for Jay Liddon." She rubbed her forehead, hoping to ease the headache that was building fast. "I'm so sorry."

"This man works for an insurance company?" Amanda asked. "And he thinks Mr. Liddon has committed fraud?"

Kaylee nodded. "But he didn't have any proof yet, although he discovered that Jay has gambling debts."

"He does?"

Kaylee frowned, trying to untangle the guesses that muddied the waters from the facts. "Maybe Joseph filed a few smaller false claims to help with his son's debt, and then he got wind of the fact that he was being investigated. So, he planned a bigger theft—either committing the crime himself or maybe asking his son to do it—to get the gambling debts paid while the authorities focused on *you*."

Amanda looked bewildered. "Do you really think so?"

Kaylee paced around the worktable. "It was Joseph's idea to let you lock the safe for the first time that night, right?"

"Yes, he'd always locked the safe himself before." Amanda sighed. "I thought it was a sign he'd grown to trust me. Apparently not."

Kaylee glanced at her watch. "I think we might be onto something, but right now I have to take a box of crafts to DeeDee's. She and Jess are setting up the Petal Pushers booth soon, and they want a good selection of items on display right away." She hoisted a large box into her arms. "Let's go, Bear."

The dog raced out of the room and flew down the stairs.

Kaylee and Amanda followed. When they got downstairs, Bear was already waiting at the front door. He gave them a doggy smile and wagged his tail.

Amanda held the box while Kaylee snapped on Bear's leash.

Kaylee took the box back from her and said, "I'll give you and Madison a ride to the bazaar. We can all go together."

Amanda hesitated. "Okay, I'll go, but I'll duck outside at the first sign that my presence is hard on Madison."

"Fair enough. I need to go a little early to drop off the rest of the crafts at the Petals' booth, but I imagine Madison has to show up early too."

"Yes, although I took all their potted plants over to the school gym already." She laughed. "I kept having visions of those carnivorous plants coming to life like some B movie, then reaching over the seat to strangle and devour me."

Kaylee smiled, admiring Amanda for keeping a sense of humor at such a trying time. *A merry heart doeth good like a medicine.*

The high school parking lot held a couple dozen cars when Kaylee, Amanda, and Madison arrived at the bazaar. Bear had sulked when Kaylee dropped him off at home.

On the far side of the lot, a car wash was set up for shoppers to get their vehicles clean while they shopped.

"They should make good money," Kaylee said.

Amanda shivered. "But getting wet sounds cold."

After Kaylee parked, she and Amanda grabbed two boxes of crafts from the trunk, and the trio trekked across the lot into the building.

Inside the gym there was a whirlwind of noise and movement. The cavernous room that usually smelled like gym socks had been transformed into an energetic bazaar with a pumpkin spice aroma.

As Kaylee gazed around, she marveled at how the autumn-colored light bulbs, dangling streamers, and twinkling white lights contributed to the festive atmosphere. Add the smell of fresh popcorn, some lively music, and jostling crowds, and it reminded her of a carnival. She found herself caught up in the excitement and hoped her friends were too.

Madison led Kaylee and Amanda to her booth, where Chloe was already waiting. The girls pushed two card tables together and covered it with a green cloth. Soon they were arranging their three types of carnivorous plants in several tiers built with bricks.

"Great idea," Kaylee said, hoping Chloe would stick around after all to wait on customers.

Amanda snapped a photo as Chloe spread out the colorful brochures and Madison tacked up the price sheets on both tables.

"Let's get the crafts to the Petals' booth." Kaylee motioned for Amanda to follow her.

Pushing through the crowd, Kaylee made sure Amanda was close behind. As they passed various booths, Kaylee spotted colorful ceramics made by students from the Art Attack classes and helium balloons for all occasions. Three high school boys had constructed a dunk tank and were filling it with colored foam balls instead of water. A dozen or more tables had been set aside for the high school science students. Madison's display was one of the most interesting, and her brochures were outstanding, if Kaylee did say so herself.

Ronald Borton was on a ladder rehanging twisted orange and purple streamers that had fallen down. Kaylee wondered if he worked for the school too or if he just helped out for special occasions.

At the far end of the gym, she noticed Penelope and Andrew coming through the door together. Was Sylvia with them? It was hard to tell as they disappeared into the crowd.

Kaylee finally found the Petal Pushers' booth. "We're here!" She waved at DeeDee and Jessica. "The booth looks great."

"It does," Amanda chimed in.

DeeDee took a bow. "Thanks. Jess and I set it up pretty fast. I think our crafts are outstanding." She lifted the long table skirt. "The sales tables are full enough, so if you two want to slip your boxes under here, we'll refill the tables from them as we sell things."

Jessica was perched on a tall stool behind the table. Her crutches poked out from under the long tablecloth, but she moved them so Kaylee and Amanda could slide their boxes under the table.

"How's your ankle?" Amanda asked.

"It's a nuisance," Jessica grumbled. "The swelling won't go down and stay down."

DeeDee shook a finger at her. "That's because you didn't keep it elevated like you were supposed to."

"How can I get anything done sitting around with my leg up?" Jessica retorted.

Kaylee laughed. If the doctor had convinced Jessica to stay home more than one day with her ankle raised, he had been more successful than most people.

"Didn't the corn-husk dolls turn out cute?" DeeDee moved some of the smallest ones toward the front. "There are individual dolls, some pairs, and a few families, complete with mothers holding babies."

Amanda pointed to a little doll swing and the tiny doll wagon. "Who made these?"

"I convinced my husband to work on them," DeeDee said. "I wish he'd had time to do more, but I thought of the idea too late."

"I bet they sell the minute the bazaar opens." Kaylee examined a doll with a flowered apron and a matching bonnet. "Who made the charming little clothes?"

"My girls did," DeeDee said. "They're always making doll clothes, and they loved doing this."

Amanda grinned. "Look at the little boy dolls with bib overalls. Oh, and the miniature broom the mother is holding."

Kaylee agreed that the corn-husk dolls were cute, but she hoped the harvest candles and flint corn wreaths sold out too. They'd bring in considerably more money for their chosen charity. "When should I take my shift here?"

"How about helping out during the second half?" DeeDee asked. "We should send Jess home by eight o'clock."

"I'm not going home that early," Jessica protested.

Kaylee squatted down and examined Jessica's ankle. "You've been on your feet all day, haven't you? Your ankle is so swollen." She stood. "Can you put your foot up on that box there?"

"I could, but I'm not going to," Jessica muttered. "You guys stop babying me."

Kaylee backed off. "Okay, but DeeDee's right. I'll take your spot at eight and work till nine or until we sell out, whichever comes first."

Jessica grabbed Kaylee's hand. "I'm sorry. I didn't mean to bite your head off."

Kaylee squeezed back. "No problem."

Amanda nudged her. "I'd like to see if Madison needs anything."

"I'll come too." They headed across the gym, the blinking lights overhead making Kaylee's red shirt glitter.

"Hey, look." Kaylee pointed at the carnivorous plant table. Even though the bazaar wouldn't officially begin for five minutes, Penelope was the first customer in line. Soon she was proudly carrying her Venus flytrap around, showing it to several people and pointing back to the girls' booth.

"That's the best kind of advertising," Amanda said. "Penelope is one sweet lady."

"Yes, she is," Kaylee agreed, "and I think Madison's going to be very busy soon. I wish Chloe had stuck around to help her."

"I think she only promised to help set up," Amanda pointed out.

True, but Kaylee thought that last-minute decision seemed irresponsible and unkind. Standing on tiptoe, she searched the gym. The crowd was thickening by the minute. The only light in the gym came from the illuminated displays and the strings of white Christmas lights draped from the ceiling and the basketball backboards.

Kaylee and Amanda stood to the side while Madison dealt with a line of eager customers. She answered questions, made change, and handed out brochures. Between customers, Madison chased away little boys who kept touching the flytraps to make them snap shut.

When the initial crowd thinned a bit, Amanda moved in closer to the table. "Your plants are selling fast. Can I help you with anything?"

Madison rattled her metal cashbox. "I'll need more change from the science teacher soon." She scanned the crowds. "And where did Chloe go? I hoped I'd convinced her to stay and help. But she disappeared just before it got busy."

"I'll go look for her," Amanda said. "I'll check the restrooms too. Maybe she's not feeling well."

Kaylee got change for Madison and helped replenish the table with plants. When she was done, she scanned the gym. At the booth next to Madison's, Ronald was delivering buckets of ice for a pink lemonade and punch stand. Penelope and Sylvia strolled arm in arm the length of the gym. And there was Andrew, under the bleachers talking to someone. Kaylee squinted to see better. Was that Chloe with him?

Andrew said something to Chloe, and she finally nodded

and headed back toward the carnivorous plant table. What had Andrew said to her? Whatever it was, Kaylee was thankful it had worked.

"There you are," Madison said when Chloe joined her. "I could use some help here."

"Sorry." Chloe glanced at Kaylee.

Kaylee pretended not to notice as she busied herself straightening the brochures on the girls' table.

"Where did you go?" Madison asked.

Chloe avoided her gaze. "I thought you'd sell more if I moved away from the table."

"What? Why?" Madison sounded genuinely puzzled.

"You know why."

"I don't. Just tell me."

Kaylee felt awkward overhearing their conversation, so she cleaned up some dirt spilled on the gym floor.

Chloe shook her head, making her earrings dance. "I know people say that I'm weird. Maybe I am." She inspected the gym, as if searching for someone. "But your mom's different. She's my friend, so I'm going to tell you something I know."

Kaylee caught Chloe's last sentence and paused. She held her breath, not wanting to miss a word, but she had trouble hearing them above the noise of the dunk tank booth.

Chloe's voice was barely discernible. "I *know* your mother didn't steal that jewelry."

"I know she didn't too. My mom would never do that."

"No, I mean I *know*."

Madison gripped Chloe's arm. "What are you saying?"

"I saw something suspicious at the jewelry store," she hissed. "I think I know who stole the jewelry."

"Who?"

Before Chloe could answer, two girls pushed to the front of

the booth. Laughing and pointing, they demanded to be shown the Venus flytrap eating a bug.

Chloe started to edge away, and Madison called to her to wait. More customers lined up at her booth, and Chloe continued to walk away.

Madison looked frantic, torn between waiting on her customers and running after Chloe. "Chloe, don't go."

Chloe glanced back and shrugged.

Madison raised her voice. "Will you meet me at the sculpture park tomorrow morning at nine? We could talk then. Please."

"I . . . I guess so," Chloe said, then disappeared into the crowd.

Had Chloe seen anything useful? Or was she planning to throw suspicion on someone else? After all, Chloe couldn't be sure that Amanda wouldn't reveal her secret—that Chloe *wasn't* home sick the day of the robbery. Far from it. She'd been at the jewelry store just before closing time.

If the missing jewelry ever *did* show up, Chloe's fingerprints might be all over it.

15

Kaylee checked her watch. When she reached the Petal Pushers booth for her shift at eight, nearly two-thirds of the long table was empty. She lifted the table skirt to retrieve the boxes of crafts. "Should I refill the display?"

"You can't." Jessica clapped. "We've already emptied all the boxes. What you see is everything that's left."

"Fantastic." Kaylee scanned the display. "You sold all but two of the corn-husk dolls? I never would have predicted that."

"Mostly kids bought them," DeeDee said. "Groups of middle school girls or smaller girls with their mothers."

Jessica grabbed her crutches. "I feel like a wimp, but I think I'll head home now." She shook her head in disgust. "Nobody tells you that after the swelling goes down the first time, it returns when you get back to normal life."

DeeDee flattened the empty cardboard boxes and stacked them on the floor. "Do you want some help to the car?"

"No, it's not that bad." Jessica waved a crutch at her. "I just like to moan and groan when I have an audience."

But DeeDee walked with Jessica anyway, clearing a path to the exit and then holding the heavy gym doors open for her.

Kaylee spread out the remaining items for sale so the table appeared fuller. If any of the candleholders or wreaths made of flint corn were left at the end of the bazaar, she'd take them to The Flower Patch and sell them there. By the time the fall festival weekend was over, Kaylee believed all their crafts would be sold. Sandra Cameron would be thrilled with the money they'd raised for the Island Grove charity project.

The aroma of caramel apples on this side of the gym made Kaylee's mouth water. She contemplated buying one.

"I know what you want," sang a merry voice.

Kaylee glanced up at Penelope and grinned. "How do you know what I want?"

"You were licking your lips and staring at those caramel apples on a stick." Penelope turned to Andrew who stood beside her. "Wasn't she?"

Kaylee slapped a hand over her heart. "Guilty as charged."

"I'll get you one," Andrew said and waved away her protest. "I was going to pick up some for Penelope and me anyway."

Penelope watched him leave, then leaned over the table. "Andrew said you're helping Amanda's lawyer track down the real jewelry thief, so I thought you'd want to know this."

"What?" Kaylee asked, her attention riveted on Penelope.

"Jeannie Drucker—you know, the Friends of the Library chairwoman—well, she heard a very reliable rumor that Joseph Liddon has put both his house and The Velvet Box up for sale."

Kaylee's hopes deflated as quickly as they'd swelled. She'd started that rumor herself.

"Jeannie said he found a buyer privately, so he doesn't have to pay fees to a real estate agent. And there would be no sale signs posted, making it easy to sell and leave town quietly." Penelope tilted her head to one side. "What's the matter?"

Kaylee sighed. "I'm afraid that rumor got started when I asked Douglas Miller at Orcas Island Realty if Mr. Liddon's home or business might be up for sale. It sounds like the rumor boomeranged back on me."

"But Jeannie was so sure," Penelope insisted. "Doesn't that sound suspicious to you? I mean, he's cutting and running after accusing Amanda."

"But I talked to Douglas Miller just this week. He said no

property for Joseph Liddon was listed, not through his office and not on the big multiple listing."

"Maybe they were listed for sale after you spoke to Mr. Miller."

"Well, that's possible, I suppose. A private sale does sound logical." Kaylee shrugged. "I guess only time will tell."

DeeDee and Andrew arrived back at the Petal Pushers' booth at the same time, and DeeDee eyed his caramel apples. When Andrew said they were almost sold out, DeeDee rushed off to buy one for herself.

Kaylee thanked Andrew for the treat and took a big bite out of her caramel apple. Andrew and Penelope started eating theirs too.

A woman with her husband in tow, both his arms full of purchases, stepped up to the Petals' table.

Kaylee set her apple down on a napkin and wiped her hands, then tapped Penelope's arm. "Don't go away."

For five minutes the determined customer tried to persuade Kaylee to lower the price on the biggest floral arrangement left for sale.

"All the proceeds go to the Island Grove charity foundation, and we want to do our best for them," Kaylee said firmly.

Finally, the woman grudgingly paid it. Her pique became petulance when she realized she would also have to carry it as her husband's arms were full.

Kaylee added the check to the cashbox, then shook her head after the woman left.

"It takes all kinds to make a world," Penelope commented.

"No kidding." Kaylee glanced around and lowered her voice. "I wanted to ask if your friend heard when the Liddons planned to move."

"She didn't know, but apparently the family is moving to a bigger house over on San Juan."

Kaylee finished her apple and licked the caramel from her sticky fingers. *I bet Mr. Liddon is in financial trouble and he's moving somewhere less expensive, not more so.* During the time Amanda had worked there, she'd once remarked that she was glad she didn't work on commission because they had far more lookers than buyers.

Andrew cleared his throat. "Penny, I think I'll go see if Madison needs any assistance."

As he walked away, Penelope whispered, "Isn't he sweet?" Then she followed him.

Kaylee smiled as she watched them go. *Smitten.*

She pondered Penelope's news. Her instincts told her that this sudden double sale—if the rumor was true—meant the Liddons were in financial trouble. She suspected the insurance money was essential to bail them out.

But how could she prove it? Her instincts were worth less than nothing in a court of law. If only she hadn't caused the private eye's identity to be exposed. Guilt swept over her at the memory of the humiliating scene when he'd caught and confronted her for blowing his cover.

An hour later the bazaar wound to a close. DeeDee and Kaylee were thrilled that they'd sold everything except one small candleholder and one large wreath. Many of the other booths had done just as well, although the white elephant auction and the ceramic cats and dogs table still had a lot left over. After cleaning up their booth, Kaylee went in search of Amanda. She was helping Madison fold up her card tables and tablecloths.

"Kaylee, I sold every plant we brought!" Madison pointed to the empty wooden trays. "And all the brochures are gone too. My teacher even took one of your scientific brochures for himself."

"Great! I'm glad it was so successful." Kaylee studied the

streamers and lights hanging from the ceiling and basketball hoops. "Do we need to stay and help clean up the rest?"

"No, we just have to take home anything we brought." Madison pulled tape off the back of her posters.

As they headed home, Kaylee loved hearing the lighthearted sound of Madison chatting with her mom. She considered telling Amanda that Joseph might be leaving town, but she decided to wait until she knew something concrete. Her rumor was no more confirmed than whatever news Chloe planned to reveal tomorrow morning. Besides, she didn't need to remind them of their troubles at the moment, not when they were so happy.

Kaylee kept waiting for Madison to bring up Chloe's mysterious message, but she didn't. Maybe Madison didn't want to get her mom's hopes up yet and didn't want to ruin the moment either. With a bit of luck, Madison would learn information that would blow Amanda's case wide open.

"Good night, ladies." Kaylee waved at them and waited till they got inside their house, then backed out of their driveway.

She swung through downtown Turtle Cove on the way home. Most cars were clustered around The Ideal Meal, the restaurant with the best steak and seafood in town. Tonight they were featuring fall festival discounts on crab bisque, seafood chowder, and crab cakes. Main Street was nearly deserted, although Death by Chocolate was open for dessert. Thankfully Jessica could leave Gretchen in charge tonight.

Kaylee ended up parking across the street from The Velvet Box. She pulled forward until the streetlight was behind her and the driver's seat was in darkness. Engine off, she sat in silence, barely aware of her own breathing. Except for the fact that Bear would bark, she wouldn't have minded having some company on this spooky errand.

Turning sideways in her seat, she stared across the street.

The jewelry store's front lights were off, but the interior of the store was more brightly lit than usual. Someone was moving around inside.

It was probably the janitor cleaning, but hadn't she seen Ronald still in the gym when she left? Maybe Jay was in there, seeing what else he could steal before the store was sold. Or maybe it was Joseph himself. Kaylee hadn't seen any of the Liddon family at the bazaar. What better time to be in the shop unobserved than when most stores downtown were closed?

Kaylee's neck muscles cramped from twisting sideways, and she massaged the knot in her neck. No one could see her where she was parked, but she couldn't see anything helpful either.

"What am I doing here?" she whispered. "I need to just check it out or go home."

Since she'd blown the private eye's cover, she really had no choice. She had to try everything she could while there was still time. She slipped her keys into her coat pocket, locked her car, and crossed the street, her footsteps muffled. A shudder ran through her, part nerves and part cold October wind. She stayed in the shadows, then took a deep breath and peeked around the edge of the jewelry store window.

It was only Ronald, and he was shampooing the carpet. He must have left the gym sooner than Kaylee thought. Was he preparing the store for a sale? Otherwise, surely the heavy cleaning would have been finished before the fall festival. She waited out of sight in case someone else was also in there. She'd love to catch a glimpse of Jay if he was anywhere around.

For a few minutes, she listened to the drone of the carpet cleaner. Finally, Kaylee closed her eyes in defeat and leaned her shoulder against the brick building. She should admit she was on a wild-goose chase and go home.

Without warning, a bony finger dug into her shoulder.

Kaylee gasped and jumped, hitting the plate glass window. She whipped around to find the night security guard, Thomas Rider, towering over her. "You scared me!"

"Sorry." He stared down at her and didn't seem the tiniest bit apologetic. "May I ask what you're doing here?"

Kaylee ran several possible explanations through her mind, but she had no reason or justification she could give him. She shrugged.

He moved a step closer. "It's not very clever to hang around after hours at a store that was recently robbed." He squinted down at her. "Especially when you're close friends with the woman arrested for the burglary."

Kaylee gritted her teeth, insulted by his insinuation, but in all honesty, she couldn't blame him. If she were the security guard, she would find her behavior suspicious too.

She might as well salvage something from this encounter and ask him a few questions. The worst he could do was tell her to get lost. "A few days ago, my friend fell from the fire escape in the alley behind the jewelry store."

"I heard about that. Snooping doesn't pay, and it's a downright foolish undertaking for grown women."

Kaylee breathed deeply and ignored his insult. "You were in the room over the jewelry store talking to Mr. Liddon that day."

Thomas stared blankly at her, neither confirming nor denying it.

"After you left, a young man entered the room and argued with Mr. Liddon," Kaylee continued. "Who was he?"

"I don't know who you're talking about." The security guard's eyes grew cold. "And I fail to see how any of that is your business."

"Was the young man Jay Liddon?" she persisted.

"It's time for you to move along now. I need to finish my rounds." He stepped around her and marched down the street.

She studied his retreating back for a moment, then crossed the street to her car. Her question had certainly struck a nerve. What was the security guard hiding?

Kaylee started the engine but didn't put the car into gear. The guard's words echoed in her mind, louder and more insistent with each repetition. *Snooping doesn't pay, and it's a downright foolish undertaking for grown women.*

It's true. Snooping doesn't pay, Kaylee silently agreed, fighting feelings of failure and near despair. She leaned her head back and blinked away the tears that threatened to spill over.

16

Kaylee's dreams that night were surreal. People jumped out of the dark to accost her, and cleaning crews shampooed her front lawn.

She awoke with relief on Saturday morning, dressed Bear in his matching blue argyle sweater and bow tie, and headed to work.

It was overcast, but hopefully they'd have sunshine later in the day. The fall festival weekend was jam-packed with outdoor family activities, food and games spilling into the sculpture park, and advertised sales events at many Turtle Cove businesses. Kaylee drove slowly down the street, enjoying the festive atmosphere.

Bear yipped joyfully, dashing back and forth across the back seat, trying to peer out every window at the same time.

When Kaylee drove by the sculpture park, she was temporarily stuck in traffic as cars vied for the small number of parking spots. People were already setting up children's games. Kaylee noticed one where a child could win a pumpkin by "ringing" it with a hula hoop. There were also tables for pumpkin painting and face painting. Big signs announced times for old-fashioned gunnysack races, relay races while balancing baby pumpkins on top of your head, and egg and spoon races where water balloons stood in for the eggs.

As the traffic bottleneck loosened, she passed the park and saw miniature golf, a family photo booth, and a church-sponsored treasure hunt. She hadn't spotted Chloe or Madison, but she hadn't expected to. It was only eight thirty.

Kaylee laughed when she neared the flower shop. "Oh, Bear, look at this."

The dachshund pressed his nose against the window and stared at the pink cotton candy truck parked right in front of The Flower Patch.

Kaylee grinned. She couldn't fight that. The enticing smell would drive her nuts all day, but it should also attract plenty of people to her shop.

Shortly after Kaylee and Bear entered the store, the bell over the door chimed.

Bear barked once. He trotted over to Amanda and leaned against her leg.

Amanda smiled and petted the dog, then hung up her jacket. "I had no idea the celebration would be so big."

"I'm glad to see the whole town getting involved, but I do think putting the cotton candy truck on my doorstep is taking unfair advantage. Cotton candy is my weakness."

Amanda grabbed a dustcloth and wiped down the counter and window ledges. "I hope those clouds don't develop into anything. I heard the forecast this morning. There's a chance of brief showers early in the afternoon."

"Then there's also a chance it won't rain." Kaylee surveyed the shop. "Feel free to say no to this, but are you in the mood to make more corn-husk dolls? Can you believe how they sold out last night?"

"I admit I was really pleased," Amanda said. "I'll put together some more for your shopwindow if you like."

"I'll take as many as you want to do. I bet we can sell them at the craft show in the park this afternoon or right here in the shop."

"If there's time before noon, I'll make a few little accessories too, like some brooms and clothing."

"You've put in more hours on these crafts than the regular Petal Pushers. I'll be sure to inform Sandra Cameron of that fact."

"There's no need. It's enjoyable work, and it's helped take my mind off things."

Kaylee waited for Amanda to mention Madison's whereabouts. Finally, she asked as innocently as she could, "Is Madison sleeping in today?"

"No, she'll be here pretty soon. She asked me to drop her off at the sculpture park to check on the placement of their plant table."

"I thought they sold out all their plants last night."

"They sold everything they'd repotted, but they saved one tray for this afternoon. That reminds me. I'd better get them out of the car." Amanda sighed. "I hope Madison doesn't expect the organizers to place the girls' table in a prominent spot. It was very nice of them to let the girls participate, but I expect they'll be on the outer fringe somewhere."

Kaylee nodded. Apparently, Madison hadn't told her mom the real reason she went to the park. Kaylee didn't blame her for not wanting to get her mom's hopes up. Chloe wasn't the most reliable girl. If she didn't show, it wouldn't be the first time.

As Amanda left to go to her car, Penelope and Andrew came in.

Bear greeted them with a bark.

"We're here to help," Penelope said. "Last night we told Madison that we'd repot some more plants this morning."

"That's nice of you," Kaylee said. "But doesn't Sylvia want you at the shop?"

"Yes. I'll only stay half an hour. Sylvia's already there, and it's not busy yet."

Kaylee couldn't help but wonder how Sylvia felt about Andrew's attentions toward her sister. Judging from some earlier comments, Sylvia wasn't too impressed with him. Kaylee reminded herself that it was none of her business and pushed the thoughts away.

When Amanda returned with the plants, they all went up to

the workroom. Penelope and Andrew formed an assembly line as they separated the delicate plants, filled cups with potting soil, and labeled each cup as a flytrap, a cobra lily, or a sundew. Kaylee caught occasional private smiles between them, and it warmed her heart.

Amanda got to work sorting and trimming softened corn husks to make more dolls. Bear curled up at her feet and fell asleep.

Kaylee slipped downstairs and stepped out on the porch, amazed again at the flood of people up and down Main Street. The chamber had done some fantastic advertising. People were already starting to gather, setting up folding chairs for the ten o'clock parade. She took a deep, mouthwatering breath of air. If she didn't go back inside soon, her resistance to the cotton candy would be shot.

A few minutes later the shop bell chimed. Three ladies bustled in and headed for the handmade soaps and lotions. Kaylee was helping them choose a gift for someone in the hospital when Reese popped in.

He held up a paper bag with the Death by Chocolate logo on it. "Chocolate chip muffins," he mouthed.

"Lifesaver," she replied in kind.

He grinned and nodded, then took the steps two at a time up to the workroom.

Kaylee ended up selling the ladies a huge gift basket of DeeDee's soaps and a get-well bouquet from the cooler. Gerbera daisies were cheery, and green button poms and lush greens created an arrangement that exuded a bright energy.

When they left with their purchases, Kaylee waved goodbye and hurried to the workroom, hoping Reese had saved her a muffin.

"Good thing I bought extra." He smiled and handed her the pastry sack. "I didn't realize you'd still be in production." He nodded at the carnivorous plants.

Kaylee thanked him and took a big bite of the soft muffin. "Did they tell you how well the high school bazaar went last night? They're scrambling to have things to sell at the park this afternoon."

Amanda deftly attached a tiny broom to her corn-husk doll. She was an old pro at the craft now. "You two are so kind to help Madison." She glanced at the clock. "She said she'd be here by now. I wonder what's keeping her."

Penelope patted Amanda's arm. "She probably ran into a friend or got sidetracked at the funnel cake truck." She smiled. "I know I would be."

Kaylee thought she might burst from knowing the real reason Madison went to the park. She didn't want to spoil things, but if Madison didn't show up soon, Kaylee wondered if someone ought to look for her.

She finished her muffin and said to Reese, "While you're here, could you check the seal on one of my coolers? It's four degrees too warm, and if it climbs higher, I could lose some flowers."

"Sure." He followed her to the first floor. "Which cooler is it?"

"None of them," she whispered.

Reese cocked one eyebrow. "You just wanted to get me alone?"

"No!" Kaylee's face flushed. "I mean, yes, but it's not like that."

He grinned at her. "What is it then?"

Kaylee filled him in on the reason Madison went to the sculpture park. "Would you mind driving past after you leave and see if you spot her?"

"No problem. Don't worry."

"Thank you. I really appreciate it."

Reese left, and Penelope left soon after. Kaylee helped trim the moist corn husks into the lengths needed, then handed them to Amanda to be turned into dolls.

Questions swirled in Kaylee's mind as she worked. What was

taking Madison so long? Why wouldn't Chloe just call Madison with her information? What was so top secret? Was Chloe going to make an admission of guilt?

The door chimed, and Kaylee hurried downstairs and stopped short. "Good morning, Mr. LeMasters." *What are you doing here?*

Despite the carnival atmosphere outside, Mr. LeMasters was dressed in a suit and a button-down white shirt. "Is Amanda here?"

"Come on up to the workroom." She led him to the work area. "You and Amanda can use my office."

Amanda froze when she glimpsed the lawyer. "What is it?" When he didn't speak, she waved a hand. "You can talk in front of my friends."

Andrew cleared his throat. "I forgot to sweep the porches. I'll go do that now." He brushed potting soil off his hands and walked out of the room.

"Should I go too?" Kaylee asked.

"No. Please stay," Amanda said.

Mr. LeMasters pulled a stool away from the dirty work area and sat down, balancing his briefcase on his lap. "I heard from the district attorney early this morning. You have been offered a deal."

Kaylee grinned, tempted to give the well-dressed lawyer a high five. At last Amanda was getting a break.

"What kind of deal?" Amanda asked, almost suspiciously.

"Please understand that I'm legally bound to bring you the offer. Mr. Liddon is apparently behind it. You're being offered a lighter sentence. It would be community service but no jail time—"

Amanda jumped down off her stool. "Is this true? I'll take it. Tell them yes!"

"One moment." Mr. LeMasters straightened his tie and cleared his throat. "The offer of no jail time is on one condition—that you surrender the rest of the missing jewelry."

Amanda looked as if she'd been struck. "But I can't. Of course they would ask for the one thing I can't do."

Kaylee felt as if all the oxygen had been sucked out of the room. What was Joseph up to? Did he really believe Amanda was guilty, or was he putting on an act? His insurance company was suspicious that he'd committed fraud. Maybe they could delay the sale of the store until the mess was sorted out.

"I might have some good news," Kaylee said tentatively. "I wasn't going to tell—it's really Madison's surprise—but Mr. LeMasters should know that the real thief may be revealed soon."

Amanda wiped her eyes. "What are you talking about?"

"Last night at the bazaar, I heard Chloe tell Madison that she had information that could prove you didn't take the jewelry. The girls were to meet at the sculpture park this morning at nine."

Amanda clapped a hand over her mouth.

Kaylee leaned on the worktable. "I didn't want to wreck Madison's big announcement, but now I think you should know. Reese said he'd drive by the park and see if she was still there. I was wondering—"

The front door of the shop flew open so hard that it hit the inside wall.

Both Kaylee and Amanda jumped, and Bear dashed down the stairs to see what the commotion was.

"Mom!" Madison cried, running into the workroom area.

Andrew followed Madison inside.

Amanda reached for her daughter. "What is it? Kaylee said you might have good news for us." She held her daughter at arm's length, her eyes sparkling with expectancy. "We could use some good news right now."

Madison didn't say anything.

Amanda's smile faded, and she lifted Madison's chin to peer into her eyes. "Honey, what's wrong?"

"Madison," Mr. LeMasters interrupted, "what news did your friend have about the theft?"

"I don't know!" Madison's voice rose an octave. "She wasn't at the park. I waited and waited." She choked back a sob. "Finally, I asked that woman who's in charge if she'd seen her." Her eyes widened in panic. "She said it was on the news last night."

"What was?" Amanda asked.

"Chloe was walking home after the bazaar on the side of the road. A witness said a speeding car got too close to her. Either it hit her or she jumped back out of the way. He couldn't say for sure. She fell and hit her head on a rock." Madison took a shaky breath. "The witness called an ambulance on one of those boxes where travelers call for emergency help."

Kaylee nodded. With cell phone coverage iffy from time to time, direct-line call boxes were stationed at intervals along the busiest roads, like the one between Turtle Cove and Eastsound.

Amanda gripped Madison's arms. "How badly was Chloe hurt?"

"The woman said Chloe was taken to the Orcas Island Medical Center in Eastsound." Madison started to cry. "And she's unconscious."

"Oh no. I'm so sorry." Amanda pulled her daughter close and hugged her, resting her chin on top of Madison's head.

Kaylee glanced at the lawyer, her mind jumping from one possibility to another. Had it really been an accident? Or had the driver of the car been the real thief? Had he been at the bazaar and heard what Chloe said? It would have been easy to follow her home and knock her off the road.

DeeDee had said Jay Liddon loved fast cars and could be reckless. Could he have been the driver?

Mr. LeMasters took out his phone. "I'll call the hospital and see how Chloe's doing this morning. If she's well enough to talk to me, I'd like to hear firsthand whatever information she has."

Kaylee strained to overhear the attorney's phone call, but all she could make out was murmuring.

Soon he disconnected the call. "With a bit of persuasion, they got me through to Chloe's room, and her mother answered the phone. No visitors are allowed. They've put Chloe in an induced coma to give the brain swelling a chance to go down."

Madison gasped. "A coma?"

Amanda hugged her. "The doctors just want her to be more comfortable right now, like when you're put to sleep for oral surgery or having your appendix out."

Mr. LeMasters nodded. "Chloe is still unconscious, but she's holding her own."

Kaylee clenched her fists. *Holding her own.* Ambiguous words, considering she was still unconscious. *Hold on, Chloe.*

17

There wasn't a sound in the flower shop for a full minute. Madison huddled in the circle of her mother's hug and cried. Even Bear seemed to sense that something was wrong. He eyed Mr. LeMasters suspiciously and circled Kaylee's legs a few times before settling down at her feet.

How exactly had Chloe landed in the medical center last night? Kaylee couldn't help but think her accident was tied to the robbery. The timing was too coincidental to be anything else.

Had Chloe seen Jay in the jewelry store one day when she was there? Had she witnessed him slipping a necklace or a couple of rings into his pocket when Joseph's back was turned? Had Chloe made the mistake of telling someone, and it got back to Jay—maybe even when she'd told Madison just the night before? Surely Chloe hadn't tried to confront him by herself. If so, had she been forced off the road because of it?

Jay had sideswiped a young girl back in high school. Last night's accident *could* have been a result of reckless behavior again, but Kaylee feared it had been a deliberate hit.

In the silence, spirited tunes by the high school's marching band echoed from the festival parade. "The Stars and Stripes Forever" contrasted sharply with the somber mood in the flower shop.

Mr. LeMasters left, and little was said as the others slowly returned to corn-husk dolls and plant repotting. A dark cloud had descended over them, and Kaylee's forced cheerful comments fell on deaf ears. Finally, she gave up trying to make conversation and worked quietly.

The room might be silent, but her mind wouldn't stop trying to figure things out. What could she do?

Then Kaylee remembered the notice in the newspaper about the Liddons' twenty-fifth wedding anniversary. The reception was to be held this afternoon at The Ideal Meal between twelve and two. It gave her an idea.

Kaylee cleared her throat. "I need to run an errand, but I'll be back shortly. Madison, could you watch Bear for me?"

Madison smiled. "Sure." She knelt down. "Come here, Bear."

While Madison cuddled the dog, Amanda glanced up at Kaylee and whispered, "Thank you."

Kaylee nodded. She knew from her own experience that hugging Bear could help most kinds of heartache.

Kaylee left by the back door and hopped into her SUV. She hadn't been able to track down Jay so far, but if he was in town, he'd be at his parents' big celebration. Finally—hopefully—she would have a chance to talk to him and get some answers.

The first question she wanted answered was this: Where had Jay Liddon been last night when Chloe was critically injured?

When she arrived at The Ideal Meal, she noticed the parking lot was crowded. It looked like the Liddons had a good turnout for their reception. Kaylee ran a comb through her hair and brushed dog hair off her shirt. Then she slung her purse over her shoulder, locked the car, and dropped her keys into her purse.

Kaylee strode into the restaurant and tried to act as if she belonged at the party.

The hostess greeted her and pointed Kaylee to the private dining room.

Framed photos of Orcas Island scenes lined both sides of the hallway: people climbing mountains, hiking the trails, watching orca whales leap out of the water, walking the beaches, dining on seafood, and visiting a local winery.

The closed double doors at the end of the hall led to the private dining room. A guest book lay open on a table with an orchid arrangement and a framed photo of the Liddons. From inside echoed the driving beat of dance music. It wasn't the kind of music Kaylee would have guessed Joseph would choose.

At the sound of footsteps behind her, Kaylee drifted away and stared out the window overlooking a courtyard. She waited until the well-dressed couple signed in. Kaylee's courage sagged as she realized just how underdressed she was. She hadn't expected guests in jeans, but neither had she expected people in sequined dresses and glittering jewels.

After the couple opened the reception doors and went in, Kaylee stuck her head inside for a peek. In the dim lighting, she could make out a spotlight at one side shining on a head table undoubtedly reserved for the Liddons and their closest friends. Before the door closed, she spotted a slightly raised platform holding a four-piece band.

She couldn't crash the party, but standing out in the hallway wouldn't get her very far either. She had to know if Jay was in there. After what Kaylee had learned from the private investigator, she had a strong feeling that Jay was a pivotal player. But how could she find out? If only there was a way to spy on the party without being seen.

Wait! There is.

When Kaylee delivered flowers here, she carried them in the back door and walked through the kitchen. The swinging door leading from the kitchen to the private dining room had a small window in it.

Hurrying down the hall, she rounded the corner leading to the kitchen entrance. Trying to walk with purpose, she entered the kitchen, nodded at the cook and a couple of waitresses, and went to stand by the swinging door. She hoped that if anyone recognized her, they'd assume she was checking on the flower arrangements in the dining room.

Through the small window, Kaylee scanned the faces of the guests at the round tables nearest her, but she didn't recognize a soul. That was highly unusual for a town as small and intimate as Turtle Cove. Had Joseph only invited people who also owned jewelry stores? Or were these guests people who had bought expensive jewelry from him over the years? Many of the women were dripping in precious gems.

Each table held an ice bucket cradling a bottle of champagne. Her mouth watered at the sight of lobster frittata, crab truffles, and fresh oysters. Even the centerpieces, mostly orchids—*not* from The Flower Patch, she noticed sourly—were the most expensive available. This reception had cost Joseph Liddon a pretty penny. How could he afford all this if he was having financial problems?

Kaylee leaned closer to the small window to get a better view of the head table. If Jay was anywhere in the room, she was sure he'd be there. The long table was decorated with huge vases of *Hydrangea arborescens*. Kaylee didn't think she'd ever seen such big hydrangea blooms. The Annabelle's white flowers were about ten inches wide.

A grand cake stood ready to be cut by the celebrating couple. The photograph beside it showed that it was a replica of the one they'd had at their wedding, which Kaylee had to admit was a nice touch.

To the left of the cake sat Mrs. Liddon, looking uncomfortable. Her smile was frozen in place as Joseph called to guests at nearby tables and totally ignored his wife.

Mrs. Liddon could have conversed with the person on her other side if there had been one. But that seat—the only unoccupied one at the head table—was empty.

Kaylee glanced down the length of the head table, but

no one there was young enough to be Jay. Her spirits sagged. Apparently, Jay hadn't shown up for his parents' anniversary reception after all.

Just then the music jolted to an end, and the lead guitarist announced a short break. The smattering round of applause for the band was lukewarm.

Kaylee guessed the response was partly relief from the insistent beat of the drums and the screeching of the electric guitars. What had possessed the pompous Joseph Liddon to invite such distinguished, wealthy guests and then entertain them with a band more suited to a night down on the wharf?

And then she saw why.

The drummer, dressed as informally as Kaylee, shook his long hair back over his shoulder and wended his way to the head table. While the other band members disappeared out a back door, the drummer swaggered over and plopped down next to Mrs. Liddon. She smiled and kissed his cheek, but he pulled away.

Jay Liddon in the flesh. Kaylee eyed him with both interest and suspicion. Maybe the only way the Liddons could entice their son to show up was if they hired his second-rate band.

Kaylee stepped back quickly as a waitress left with pitchers of ice water, moving aside so the swinging door didn't hit her. At least she knew now that Jay was in town, but how could she speak to him? After eating, would he resume playing while the Liddons cut the cake and made speeches? She couldn't hang out in the kitchen for that long.

Maybe she could wait in the parking lot until the party broke up. He might even get bored and leave early.

Then an unwelcome thought struck her. What if that wasn't Jay Liddon? Mrs. Liddon had kissed him, but that was no proof. High-society people frequently kissed friends on the cheek. She needed to know for sure, or this was a waste of time.

She waited as the waitress returning with empty pitchers pushed into the kitchen. When the door swung back, Kaylee slipped into the dining room with her heart pounding. Holding her breath, she shrank back against the wall, motionless in the subdued lighting.

She slid her phone from her purse and used the camera to zoom in on the young man sitting by Mrs. Liddon. He really didn't look much like the yearbook photo. Of course, that photograph of the clean-cut angular face had been taken five years ago. Could it be the same face as the drummer's? The man's features appeared as if he were going soft from years of hard living and hard drinking. His eyebrows were drawn low over hooded eyes, and the bushy eyebrows contrasted oddly with his thin, scraggly mustache.

She snapped a picture of the drummer. She sent it to Jessica with the caption: *Is this Jay?* She hoped that her friend was near her phone.

Kaylee became uncomfortably aware that several heads had swiveled in her direction. She slipped back into the kitchen, smiled at the cook, and exited into the hallway. She'd just made it to the parking lot when her phone buzzed.

Jessica's text wasn't much help. *Not sure if it's Jay or not. Sorry. Hard to tell with long hair and a mustache.*

Kaylee debated her next move. She'd come too far to go back now, and time was quickly running out for Amanda. But while she fought panic, a clearer and calmer voice in her head instructed her to stop where she was. She paused and gazed around her.

If Jay was inside the restaurant, his car must be somewhere in the parking lot. And if he'd sideswiped Chloe the night before, his car could show some damage, couldn't it?

Straightening, Kaylee started down the rows of cars. She didn't know what kind of car he drove. Jay might have received a new Mustang on his sixteenth birthday, but she doubted he still had the same car, although he might have bought another sports car.

At the end of the third row, she spotted a brand-new bright red Camaro convertible with the top down. She was within twenty feet when she noticed the out-of-state license plate. Her pulse quickened.

Kaylee scanned the empty parking lot. No one was around so she crouched and walked around the car, searching for scratches or dents—anything to indicate an accident. The car had tires with deep tread. She snapped a photo. Later she'd send the photo to the sheriff and ask if the tread matched any tracks they might have spotted on the shoulder where Chloe was found injured.

She circled the car twice, but the second inspection revealed no more than the first time around. Nothing. The car was as polished and scratch-free as if it had just been driven off the salesroom floor.

"Can I help you?" someone said behind her.

Startled, she whirled around so fast she nearly fell over. It was the drummer. "Jay Liddon?"

The young man studied her as he lit a cigarette. "Who's asking?"

Kaylee didn't know how to respond. She decided to be honest and get right to the point. "I'm a local business owner, and I know your father. This is your sports car, right?"

"My dad knows a lot of people," Jay said. "And why does my car concern you?"

"The only reason I'm asking about your car," Kaylee said evenly, "is that last night a young girl walking home was forced off the road and seriously injured. She may not recover."

"So?"

She stared him down. "You have a history of sideswiping girls by the side of the road."

His eyes flashed, and he took a swift step forward. "Now why would I force some girl off the road?"

"Maybe she had information that would implicate you in the jewelry thefts."

"Have you lost your mind?" Jay asked. "Do I strike you as the type to wear emeralds and diamonds?"

"No, but emeralds and diamonds would help pay off your gambling debts." Kaylee couldn't believe her boldness, but she had to get a straight answer. She desperately needed to help Amanda.

"How did you know?" Jay snarled.

Kaylee still wasn't positive Jay had been in that upstairs room above the jewelry store when Jessica fell from the fire escape, but after hearing what the private detective had discovered, she decided to bluff. "I was in the alley and heard you yell, 'You can't do this to me' at your father. What had he done? Stopped paying off your loan sharks?"

Jay sprang forward, and Kaylee instinctively stepped backward—and collided with something.

She glanced over her shoulder to see Joseph Liddon.

18

Kaylee whirled around. "I'm sorry." She hadn't heard him cross the parking lot.

"You again! What's going on here?" Joseph's question cut the air like a machete.

Her face flaming, she backed up two feet. "I was just—"

Joseph pointed at his son. "Put out that cigarette and get back inside. And play some music that my age group can dance to."

Eyes narrowed, the young man ground out his cigarette with his boot, then swaggered toward the restaurant.

Joseph glowered at Kaylee, but he said nothing more and followed his son inside.

Weak in the knees, Kaylee hurried toward her own car, but as she crossed the lot, a sheriff's deputy car pulled into view.

Nick rolled down his window. "What's up? I was watching you." He nodded in the direction of Jay's Camaro. "It seemed like you were casing the lot for something to steal."

Kaylee rolled her eyes. "Not likely."

"You okay? You look a bit pale."

"I'm fine." She pulled out her phone. "I want to show you something." For the next few minutes, she told him about her suspicions of Jay being part of the cover-up of the jewelry theft. "And I thought you could take this photo of his tires and compare it to any prints found at the scene of Chloe Padgett's accident last night."

"Send the photo to Sheriff Maddox." Nick rubbed his hand across his chin. "I appreciate you sharing your concerns with us, and you might be right about Jay Liddon. Or you might not be. But please let the police handle the investigation."

Kaylee didn't reply. Handle the investigation? Were they still investigating, or were they satisfied that Amanda had done it?

"You're very quiet," Nick observed. "Are you upset because we arrested your friend? We have to do our jobs."

"I know."

"For your sake as well as Amanda's, I hope that she's proven innocent."

"Thanks." She smiled. *And I'm determined to see that she is.*

Disappointed, Kaylee drove back to The Flower Patch, pondering her next move. She sent the photo of Jay's car tires to Sheriff Maddox, hoping he would at least consider that Chloe might have been targeted on purpose. Hopefully Nick would follow up on it too. Even though Jay's car hadn't been scratched, he could have nudged Chloe off the road without damaging his convertible. Kaylee could tell the sheriff what she'd overheard at the bazaar, and he could decide what to do.

If he was interested, she would also give him her notes stored on her phone, although her speculations about the Liddons were just that—speculations. Even so, she wanted to share all her information with Sheriff Maddox in a concise and coherent way so he would take her ideas seriously.

Back at the shop, Bear eagerly met her at the door, and she scratched behind his ears. It was blessedly quiet. Andrew was alone, and Amanda had taken Madison home. With the bazaar over, she might as well take some of the quiet time and work on ideas for Kathy Fitz's Thanksgiving fund-raising event at the library.

Up in her office, she searched high and low for the notepaper where she'd scribbled ideas when on the phone with Kathy. It was nowhere on the desk or in her files, and she dug through the wastebasket next, finally dumping it on the floor in frustration and sorting through the papers one by one.

Bear padded through the papers, nose down, as if helping her search.

Sitting back on her heels, she closed her eyes and tried to think back to when she'd taken Kathy's call. She could picture the piece of paper she'd ripped off the notepad after hanging up. What had she done with it? She'd been so distracted at the time that she barely recalled any details of what Kathy wanted. She only remembered that it was for Thanksgiving and involved Pilgrims or Native Americans or maybe Plymouth Rock? It was a blur.

Something had happened right after that phone call. She'd taken the call upstairs, and Madison and Chloe had arrived at the shop unexpectedly because of early dismissal. And Kaylee clearly remembered stuffing her page of notes into her jeans pocket. The note wasn't in the pair of jeans she wore now. She seriously hoped it hadn't gone through the wash and disintegrated.

It could have fallen out of her back pocket when she was driving, so hopefully the list was in the car. She slipped out the door and jogged to her car. She searched the floor, down the sides of the seats, and underneath. Nothing. She sat back in exasperation.

"Where can it be?" she muttered.

Then Kaylee remembered. That day after work, she'd gone to the apple farm. Maybe it had worked out of her jeans pocket as she wriggled through the hole she made in the loose boards. It could still be inside the shed or in the grass behind the building. She sighed. She'd have to run out to the apple farm and try to find it.

She asked Andrew to watch the shop and Bear while she ran another errand.

Outside, she hurried back to her car. The breeze seemed a bit stronger, and it felt several degrees colder.

Across the street, Ronald swept blowing leaves away from the jewelry store's front door.

Kaylee caught his eye and yelled, "I think you're fighting a losing battle!"

Ronald laughed and walked toward her. "I think you're right." He pointed at the sky. "It seems the storm is blowing through sooner than predicted."

"I just hope it doesn't ruin the outdoor events later this afternoon and tonight." She opened her car door.

"Hope you have an umbrella."

"No, but I won't be long. I lost something at an apple farm I need to find."

"Good place to get fresh apple cider."

"It used to be, but Payne's Apple Farm isn't operational anymore. It just has special memories for me."

"Oh. Well, stay dry."

Kaylee waved and climbed into her SUV. When she arrived at the farm, she parked under a madrone tree. As she strode up the driveway, a sudden gust of wind blew dirt in her eyes. Leaves overhead rustled. Faint thunder rolled in from the west, and she picked up her pace. She didn't want to get drenched.

The shed door was still shut and barred. Kaylee searched the ground around it first, including the back side where she'd broken off the boards to get out. She combed through the tall grass but didn't find a scribbled note. She stopped for a moment to examine Reese's solid repair job. It reminded her that he hadn't sent her a bill for fixing it yet. She'd have to remind him.

At the front of the shed, she opened the door wide and peered inside. Light from the doorway fell on the workbench under the boarded-over window. On the workbench next to a pair of pruning shears was a piece of paper. Could that be her list of notes? She kicked the door open as wide as it would go, dashed inside the shed, and grabbed the paper. It was her notes!

Kaylee raced outside. As she closed and barred the door, the wind whipped her hair around her face. Something bothered her. How could she have dropped her notes so the paper landed on the workbench? It made no sense.

Thunder boomed as she started toward the car. Rumbles rolled down the mountain even louder, and she began to jog. She hustled past the garage, the cistern, and the open-sided machine shed. Everything appeared exactly as it had a few days ago. But striding past the apple barn, she halted and stared.

Was she seeing things . . . or had someone else been here?

19

Kaylee bent down to examine the faint path. When she was here earlier in the week, the overgrown grass and weeds had stood straight. Now a path at the side of the barn was matted down. Someone had walked through the tall grass more than once.

The path was too wide to have been made by an animal. Human feet had crushed and bent the grass stalks. Her gaze followed the trail to the corner of the barn. Whoever had broken into the house and the shed had found a safer place to meet.

The skin on the back of her neck tingled. Kaylee had an eerie feeling that she knew where the trail would lead if she followed it to its end.

Straightening, she tracked the curving path through the flattened grass, zigzagging around some old apple-picking equipment. Halfway across the weedy patch behind the barn and about twenty feet out, she stopped. *Right about here.* She pivoted slowly.

About ten feet away, she spotted a small pile of boards next to a depression in the ground. She inched forward.

Long grasses had grown over the edges of the hole. On hands and knees, she stared down into the blackness of the dry well. Kaylee's stomach lurched as memories washed over her of the time spent alone down there when she'd been afraid she was lost forever.

With the sky darkened, she could see only about five feet down into the hole. Three feet down, she noticed a ladder leaning against one side of the dirty well.

Lightning flashed, but Kaylee remained motionless on the edge of the well. She refused to even consider the next obvious step. Her mind was loud and insistent, shouting, "Danger!" at the sheer terror of going belowground.

She chided herself for her immature reaction, but she couldn't help but feel five years old again, trapped in the well, shouting her throat raw before her grandfather found her.

"That was then, and this is now," she told herself firmly. "It won't happen again. And there's a ladder this time."

Thunder grew louder, and huge raindrops splattered on the ground.

She needed to check it out now or hightail it to her car before she got soaked.

Kaylee aimed her phone's flashlight into the well. She caught a glimpse of a box and something else that glittered. But unless she climbed down there, she wouldn't know what she'd found—if anything.

Taking a deep breath, she forced it out with a hiss between clenched teeth. She put her phone back into her jacket pocket, then crept to the edge of the well. With her legs over the side, she tried to reach the ladder's top rung. Her legs were too short by several inches.

Kaylee turned around and knelt at the edge of the well. Lying on her stomach in the scratchy grass, she wriggled backward and dropped her legs into the hole. Her dangling feet groped for the ladder.

When her toes touched the top rung, she wriggled back farther until her full weight rested on the ladder. Peering down into the darkness, Kaylee's knees wobbled. She gripped the grassy ledge and dropped one foot to the next rung. On the fourth rung, her head reached ground level.

Rung by rung, she continued to the floor of the well. She

gazed up at the dim circle of daylight above her, and several drops of rain hit her face. She sensed the moist rocky sides of the well closing in.

Kneeling on the hard earth at the bottom, she felt around on the ground. Her hand brushed over several small objects. She reached into her pocket for her phone and turned on the flashlight again. A circle of light shone on the gray stone wall, and she felt enormous relief as the suffocating darkness was pushed back a little.

On the other hand, seeing how close the walls were on every side made the word *claustrophobia* seem alive and personal.

Pointing the light down, Kaylee squinted at several objects in a wooden box. A white piece of paper lay on top. Kaylee took the document and held it up close to the light.

The name of a pawnshop in Bellingham was printed across the top, and the transaction was dated three days earlier. Kaylee squinted and read, *One ring—2-karat center diamond, square cut, plus six smaller diamonds surrounding it, 14-karat white gold*. The price received for it was listed, but she couldn't make out the signature scrawled at the bottom.

Kaylee whistled softly. She was holding a pawnshop receipt for a ring stolen from The Velvet Box—and probably signed by the actual thief. She'd finally found proof of Amanda's innocence!

Kneeling by the box, Kaylee played the flashlight over several other objects, searching for more evidence. She lifted a round, flat object into the flashlight beam. Something stirred in her memory as she rubbed the ornate gold cover.

In a flash, she was back in the alley behind The Velvet Box, seeing Ronald check the time on a pocket watch. Unless she was mistaken, she now held that watch, the one he had claimed was given to him by his grandfather.

Suddenly weak, Kaylee leaned against the side of the well.

Ronald must be the thief. She could think of no other reason why his gold pocket watch and a pawnshop receipt were hidden in the well. Had the watch been stolen from somewhere else, and he'd given in to the temptation to wear it in Turtle Cove? Maybe after she'd remarked on the watch, he'd realized it was elegant enough to draw attention.

Kaylee inspected the rest of the floor as her mind leapfrogged from one memory to another. Ronald worked nights at the jewelry store, and he had also been at the bazaar, helping at various places in the gym. Had he overheard Chloe's plan to reveal vital information to Madison? Had Chloe seen him at the bazaar and been frightened by him? Is that why she'd run off so suddenly? Kaylee tried to remember if she'd seen Ronald after Chloe left, but she couldn't be sure.

A loud crack of thunder interrupted her dizzying thoughts. She glanced up, and two big raindrops hit her face. She'd better hurry. She flashed the light around the well one last time. It was then that she glimpsed the corner of an envelope sticking out from under the wooden box.

She pulled it out. When she removed the letter inside, a photograph fluttered to the cold floor. Retrieving the picture, Kaylee held it in front of the light. Something hazy stirred in the back of her mind. The tall, thin man in the yellowed picture seemed familiar — something about the eyes and the mouth. But the photo had been taken a long time ago.

After unfolding the brittle letter, she began to read. Her eyes widened. At the end of the letter she leaned weakly against the rough wall of the well. Now it finally made sense, including the signature on the pawnshop receipt. She stuffed the photograph and the letter into her pocket, along with the watch, and grabbed for the ladder.

In her haste, Kaylee bumped against the side of the well

and dropped her phone. A splintering sound was followed by the light blinking out.

Kaylee froze, staring up from the bottom of the gloomy well into the darkening sky overhead.

I can't be trapped down here again!

20

Kaylee fought a nearly overwhelming urge to scream, just as she had as a small girl. But Grandpa couldn't come to her rescue this time.

Calm down. I have the ladder. Take a deep breath.

Then, with horror, she remembered telling Ronald where she was going. She'd even mentioned the name of the farm.

Had Ronald followed her out here? Was he up above now, just waiting for her to crawl out of the well?

Taking a deep, shuddering breath, Kaylee dropped to her knees and swept her hands over the dirty, leaf-filled bottom of the well until she found her phone. She snatched it up and turned it on. Although she'd cracked the screen, thankfully the phone appeared to be working.

She tried to call Jessica, but there wasn't a strong enough signal to even send a text. She pocketed her phone and decided to try again when she got aboveground.

She groped for the ladder, gripped its sides, and began to climb. Her heart pounded so hard that it hurt. With each step up, rain fell on her more heavily. Her hair was soon plastered to her head.

When her head reached ground level, she scanned the area all around her. Ronald wasn't waiting, unless he'd flattened himself in the tall grass or was around the corner of the barn. Grasping each slippery rung, she climbed the last two steps and flung herself over the edge of the well into the soggy grass. Lightning flashed as she dragged her legs out of the well.

Dark sheets of rain hung from gray clouds in the west.

Kaylee ran down the driveway to her car, wiping the rain out of her eyes.

In the SUV, she locked the doors, cranked up the heater, switched on the windshield wipers, and tried to call Jessica again, even though her phone showed little charge. She waited impatiently, drying her face on a wad of tissues from the glove compartment and searching for signs of traffic on the country road.

Jessica didn't answer.

Well, she couldn't wait. She sped away from the farm and found a safe place to pull over, then called Jessica once more.

This time her friend answered at Death by Chocolate right away. "What's up? You need a dozen chocolate chip muffins delivered pronto?"

"No, something even bigger. Listen." As the windshield wipers swished and the side windows fogged over from the humidity, Kaylee explained what she'd found. "I'm heading back to the shop right now. Can you meet me there?"

"Shouldn't you call the sheriff first?"

"No, all I have is a theory with some circumstantial evidence. If I play my cards right, I hope to trick a confession out of the thief in front of several witnesses."

"Okay. Meet you there. Good luck, Sherlock."

"Thanks, Watson." She hung up, then called Amanda. "Can you stop by the shop in a few minutes? I believe I have some very good news for you, and I want to tell you in person."

"Really?" Amanda sounded surprised. "I could use some good news right now. Madison's working on her homework, but I'll be there."

After Kaylee disconnected, she phoned Penelope.

"The Chandlery Gift Shop," Penelope said brightly. "How may I help you?"

"This is Kaylee. I was wondering if you and Sylvia could stop by The Flower Patch." The sisters had grown close to Amanda and Madison and deserved to be there when the culprit was revealed. "I have a surprise that is going to make a lot of people happy." Not everyone, Kaylee knew, but that couldn't be helped.

"Oh, I love surprises. With the sudden rain, the foot traffic in the store has been sparse. I can pop over for a bit, but Sylvia will need to stay here. See you soon."

Kaylee took a shuddering breath and phoned The Velvet Box. "This is Kaylee Bleu, the owner of The Flower Patch. I'm interested in the services of the maintenance man who performs cleaning services for you. Could you give me Ronald Borton's phone number? I can't find it in the book."

"Just a moment," the young-sounding salesgirl chirped. "I'll get it for you."

Kaylee jotted down the number, then thanked the salesgirl and disconnected. One more call and then all the players would be in place. "Ronald, this is Kaylee Bleu. I'd like to talk to you about hiring your services for a month or so. Are you interested?"

He didn't hesitate. "Yes."

"Great. Could you come to the flower shop? I'll be there within ten minutes. I can show you what I need, and we can discuss wages then."

"Glad to. See you then."

Kaylee waited for her heart rate to slow down before getting back on the road. She swung by Penelope and Sylvia's house to pick something up. Then she was off again, adrenaline running so high that it almost overrode her fear.

Almost.

Kaylee parked well out of sight of The Flower Patch. Sneaking through the back door of the shop, she held her breath and waited by the coolers. Grateful that she'd used a hair dryer on the swollen door, she slipped easily into the small closet that held vases, ribbons, and other supplies. She left the door ajar, concentrating intently, identifying voices. She didn't want to appear until all the players in the little drama were present.

Jessica's lilting voice was the easiest to distinguish. Kaylee only hoped that her friend would be ready to act when needed.

"How's your ankle?" Amanda asked.

"Fine. My hubby makes me keep the crutches with me. I don't really need them now, but with the wet sidewalk and streets, they help me to not slip. It's sweet of you to ask." She paused. "Where's your lovely daughter? Out enjoying the festival food?"

"She set off to buy a stuffed animal for her friend Chloe, who just regained consciousness. We'll drop it off at the front desk if Chloe can't have visitors."

Wonderful news! Kaylee wanted to clap.

"Speaking of food," Penelope said, "what's in the bag you brought?"

A paper sack rustled. "Assorted chocolate items. Take your pick." Jessica laughed. "Today I lost count of how many customers told me chocolate jokes. I can never let on that I've heard them all a dozen times."

"Like what?" Amanda asked. "Tell us some."

"Why is there no Chocoholics Anonymous?" Jessica let them ponder it for a moment, then continued, "Because no one wants to quit."

There were a few chuckles.

"What is the twelve-step program's first rule for chocoholics?" Jessica said. "Never get more than twelve steps away from chocolate."

Penelope giggled. "That's my kind of program."

"Do you know any more?" Andrew asked.

"Oh, try this one. How do you avoid eating too much chocolate?" Jessica paused. "Melt it and drink it instead."

"This was Madison's favorite joke when she was little,"

Amanda piped up. "What is a monkey's favorite cookie?" she asked. "Chocolate chimp."

A guttural laugh prompted Kaylee to lean close to the gap in the door. That had to be Ronald. He'd come. *Good.* She needed the star of the show.

Kaylee breathed deeply, trying to still her racing heart. Now that it was time to catch the thief, her mind went blank, and she broke out in a cold sweat. She couldn't think of a single workable plan to trap Ronald. What had sounded so clever as she sat in her car now felt totally unworkable. But everyone was here, so she had to do something.

Kaylee closed her eyes, concentrating on every word she could hear as she edged the door open another inch.

"I think the forecaster got it wrong," Penelope commented.

"I hope the wind doesn't knock the booths around in the park," Jessica added.

"I'll check when the rain quits," Ronald said. "I was hired to take booths down at five to make room for the concert in the park tonight." He cleared his throat. "I saw Miss Bleu earlier. I warned her about the rain. She said she was headed out to some farm."

"An apple farm that's for sale," Jessica explained. "She dropped an important paper out there a few days ago."

"She wants to buy a farm?" Andrew asked. "You mean, to grow her own flowers?"

"No, she's not buying it," Jessica said. "She spent time there as a child. Her grandfather was good friends with Ben Payne, the man who operated Payne's Apple Farm for many years."

"Now that you mention it," Amanda said, "I wonder what's keeping her."

That's my cue. Kaylee crept out of the small closet and into view. "I'm right here," she announced, watching Ronald's startled reaction from the corner of her eye.

All five people spun to face her in surprise.

Penelope put a hand over her heart. "My goodness, you gave me a start. I didn't hear you come in."

"I came in the back way. What a shower I got caught in." Kaylee laughed self-consciously and pushed her flattened hair off her forehead.

"Did you find your notes?" Jessica asked.

"Yes, but I found something even more interesting out there. That's why I got caught in the rain." Kaylee hung up her wet coat and reached for her sweater hanging on a hook. "When I was little, I fell down an old well on the property. Today I found it again."

Amanda's eyes widened. "You didn't fall in again, did you?"

"No, I didn't *fall* in."

Ronald's eyes never left Kaylee's face.

"I didn't fall in because someone had put a ladder in the well. I just climbed down."

Although Kaylee was near Ronald, she sensed, rather than saw, him tense up. He was ready to spring, like a caged tiger at the zoo.

"Did you find anything down there?" Jessica asked.

In the sudden stillness, Kaylee could hear Ronald's ragged breathing. "Yes, believe it or not, I found proof of Amanda's innocence. I can prove who—"

Snarling, Ronald lunged at her.

21

Before Ronald could grab Kaylee, Jessica swung her crutch out. Ronald saw it too late and crashed to the floor. He grunted, then rolled over and reached for Jessica.

Kaylee sprang forward. "Amanda, help me!"

Amanda and Kaylee landed on Ronald's back and slammed him to the floor. His arms and legs were in a tangle, and Kaylee was knocked sideways by his twisting body.

"Help me, you idiot!" Ronald cried.

Gasping for air, Kaylee yelled at Penelope, "Cut some of that twine!"

Ronald thrashed on the floor, swearing. But with Amanda sprawled across his back, Kaylee pinning his legs, and Jessica poised to crack him over the head with her crutch, there was only so much he could do.

Penelope grabbed the twine and quickly bound Ronald's ankles. With another long piece, Kaylee tied his hands behind his back.

Amanda grabbed a lilac bandanna from one of the store displays. "I think that's quite enough from you." She gagged the cursing janitor and tied the ends of the bandanna firmly behind his head.

Kaylee rocked back on her heels and gasped for air. When she caught her breath, she stood and glanced around. "Where's Penelope?"

"Right here." She hurried over. "I locked your front door and flipped the sign to Closed. Should I call the police?"

"Not yet. I will in a minute." Kaylee grinned. "That was quick thinking."

Penelope shrugged. "It's part of our store's emergency plan in case of a crisis situation." She glared down at the writhing janitor. "I figured a criminal getting trussed up like a turkey qualified as an emergency." She laid a hand on Andrew's arm. "Are you okay? Your face is so pale."

He nodded. "But I can't believe this."

"It is shocking," Penelope agreed. "I'm glad Madison wasn't here. She's had enough to deal with lately."

As Kaylee sank into a chair, she glimpsed movement near the stairs. Bear peeked around the corner. She hadn't heard him come down. The commotion must have jolted him out of his dreams.

Kaylee leaned down and held out her hand.

Bear's ears perked up, and he trotted closer for a good petting. He delighted in his back scratch and looked up at her, waiting patiently while she straightened his bow tie. Then he edged over to where Ronald was tied up. The dog gave the janitor a wide berth as he went to check on the others, growling at the man in his fiercest protective manner.

Amanda sat near Ronald, looking ready to clobber him with one of Jessica's crutches. "Are you sure he did it?"

"There's no mistake," Kaylee replied. "I found concrete evidence down in the well that Ronald's our thief."

"Don't keep us in suspense," Jessica piped up. "What evidence?"

"Payne's Apple Farm was being used as a meeting place," Kaylee answered. "The real estate agent told me the house was broken into. But I never suspected Ronald was the culprit. I believed everything he told me."

Amanda frowned. "Like what?"

"For one thing, he told me who had access to the safe," Kaylee replied. "He conveniently left himself off the list, but he worked at the jewelry store after closing hours all alone. And he was at the bazaar. He could have easily overheard Chloe tell

Madison she had information about the robbery. She must have seen something."

Amanda nodded. "Chloe stopped in at the jewelry store quite often for someone her age."

"On one of those visits she must have seen Ronald do something and just last night realized its significance. We'll know soon what she witnessed." Grimly, Kaylee studied the bound man on the floor. "I don't want to believe this, but he could have followed Chloe on her way home after the bazaar and caused her injury."

"Isn't this all circumstantial?" Amanda asked. "Mr. LeMasters would say so. And the police said the safe wasn't even broken into."

Kaylee paced around the room, playing with a length of twine. "Ronald didn't have to tamper with the safe. He had help from someone with experience cracking safes." She stopped beside Andrew's chair and spoke to his bowed head. "If you promise not to run, we promise not to tie you up too."

He nodded without raising his head.

Penelope gasped. "What on earth are you saying?"

Sadly, Kaylee looked from Penelope's shocked face to Amanda's. "I told you Ronald had help. Meet his accomplice."

Amanda's mouth hung open, and Penelope's face blanched to a pasty white.

"I'm afraid it's true. Andrew is Ronald's uncle. They worked together in the jewelry theft." Kaylee pulled the gold watch from her pocket and set it on the counter.

"How do you know this?" Penelope demanded, her voice cracking.

Kaylee reached again into her pocket and pulled out the musty-smelling letter she'd found in the well. She handed the yellowed photograph to Penelope first, who then passed it to Amanda.

"Who's this?" Amanda peered closer. "Wait a minute. The younger man could be Ronald. Are you saying the tall one is Andrew?"

Kaylee nodded. "According to the notes on the back, that picture was taken nearly twenty years ago. By the way, Ronald Borton is really Ronald Goldfield, the son of Andrew's brother. And Andrew Whitaker here is really Andrew Goldfield."

Penelope stared at Andrew. "Is this true?"

Andrew wouldn't meet her eyes. "Yes, I raised him while I worked on the railroad."

"And this isn't the first time they committed a crime together. Let me read that part." Kaylee skimmed down the page. "Ronald wrote this from New Mexico right after Andrew moved here. 'Think twice before you refuse me. I need at least $20,000. Help me crack a safe on the island, or I'll go to the cops in Chicago. They still want to know who cracked the safe in that burglary. I served time, but I kept my mouth shut about you. You got off free thanks to me, Uncle. I want out of the country. Help me one more time, and then I'll disappear without a trace.'"

Jessica frowned. "So, they robbed a business in Chicago?"

Kaylee nodded. "The police won't have any trouble tracking it down." *And I should call the police soon. But first . . .* "Ronald served time for it, but since he wants to leave the country, he's no doubt committed more recent crimes."

"Why did you do it?" Penelope whispered.

"I don't expect you to understand, Penny." Andrew rubbed his smooth head with a trembling hand. "I never had enough to eat when I was a kid. I dropped out of school in the fourth grade to get a job to help my parents. Later I went north to work on the railroad where the pay was better."

His voice was so low that Kaylee had to move closer to hear.

"Then what happened?" Penelope prompted quietly.

"When Ronnie was five, my brother died. Ronnie came to

live with me. There were so many things he needed, and I wanted to give them to him. There was never enough money," Andrew said, his voice faltering. "When I got laid off from the railroad, I worked odd jobs, but it wasn't nearly enough."

"So how did you get involved in criminal activities?" Penelope asked.

Andrew cleared his throat. "Ronnie was in trouble a lot. When he was older, I worked part-time for a locksmith. He talked me into borrowing the company's safecracking equipment and using it to rob a small jewelry store. I wasn't caught. I wanted to quit while I was ahead, but Ronnie had different plans." His head sagged forward on his chest. His confession seemed to have exhausted him.

Ronald managed to spit out his soggy gag. "Cut the sob story, Uncle! You're as much to blame as I am."

Amanda stuffed the gag back into his mouth.

"When Ronald showed up in Turtle Cove, he got jobs doing janitorial work for several businesses," Kaylee explained, then faced Andrew. "Did he blackmail you into helping him with more robberies?"

Andrew nodded but didn't lift his head.

"So you planted that necklace in my house!" Amanda cried. "You're responsible for getting me arrested, for people in this town ostracizing me."

"No!" Andrew's head snapped up. "I wouldn't have done that. That was Ronnie's doing."

"No offense," Jessica said, "but I have trouble seeing Andrew here as a safecracker. And no one has mentioned ever seeing Andrew anywhere near The Velvet Box."

"I don't believe his assistance required his presence in the store." Kaylee caught Amanda's eye. "Joseph Liddon's safe was fairly old with a combination lock, right?"

Amanda nodded. "But as far as I know, nobody but Mr. Liddon had the combination."

"People often use personal information and dates for passwords and combinations to make them easy to remember," Kaylee pointed out. "Things like birthday or anniversary dates, old phone numbers or address numbers, birth dates of favorite movie stars or athletes. Things like that."

"But how would Andrew know any of those?" Amanda asked.

"He told me once that he spent much of his time at the public library. That's where Mary Bishop's husband met him," Kaylee explained. "I delivered flowers to the library and saw him poring over the society pages in the reading room. There was a notice about the Liddons' twenty-fifth wedding anniversary."

Jessica's mouth dropped open. "And from the date of their anniversary, he got the combination to his safe?"

"No, I don't think so. The anniversary announcement was in the paper after the robbery. He could have gotten information on the Liddons other ways before that. The computers give us access to all kinds of background on people." Kaylee touched Andrew's shoulder. "Did you use the library computers to discover personal information?"

Andrew shook his head. "I couldn't find anything on a computer. I hate those things."

"Then how?"

He sighed heavily. "I searched for Liddon kids in the annual yearbooks the library has. Jay Liddon graduated five years ago."

"You used his birthday numbers to get into the safe?"

"We tried, but Ronnie said that didn't work. His graduation date did, though."

Kaylee recalled the night she'd delivered flowers to the library. When Andrew had covered the newspaper, she'd been touched that he'd protected Madison from seeing the Liddons' anniversary photo. But that wasn't what he was reading, she now realized.

She also remembered a report of a birthday party for the owner of High Tide Outfitters on that page. It had included the names of Vince Mack's two children and six grandkids. Kaylee wondered if Andrew had been researching that store for their next burglary.

"Did you find the missing jewelry in the well?" Amanda asked. "Can we prove they stole it all?"

"I didn't find all the jewelry, but I discovered a receipt from a pawnshop in Bellingham." Kaylee pulled out the paper. "It says that a diamond ring was pawned, and its description is given. It matches one of the stolen rings. It took me a while to see that the signature on the ticket was Andrew's." *And he'd have to ride the ferry to get to Bellingham to visit that pawnshop, which is why he headed that way after he left the library.*

Jessica nodded. "If the ring is still at the pawnshop, that should be enough. The clerk can identify Andrew."

"If the pawnshop owner will admit to accepting it," Kaylee said doubtfully. "He'll be in trouble for buying stolen merchandise instead of contacting the sheriff's office. Even if the theft hadn't been reported to pawnshops in the area, they should have checked. This piece of jewelry would have been easy to identify."

Amanda tilted her head to one side. "I wish we could find all the jewelry. Where do you think the rest might be?"

"I believe Penelope has it," Kaylee said.

"Me?" Penelope sputtered in astonishment.

"You didn't realize it, but you're hiding the jewelry," Kaylee told her. "Everyone, wait here while I get something I left outside the back door."

In a moment she was back with a large pot containing a northern maidenhair fern that was a bit droopy. Kaylee carefully dumped the *Adiantum pedatum* out of the pot onto the counter.

Pebbles from the bottom of the pot mixed in with the light-colored, very crumbly soil.

Kaylee poked a finger through the dirt, brushed the soil from three small plastic bags, and held them up for everyone to see. Through the dirty plastic, two shiny rings and two beautiful necklaces were visible.

"I'm sorry, Penelope," Kaylee said. "When Andrew surprised you by repotting your fern, he took the opportunity to hide the stolen jewelry in your pot. He must have assumed the jewelry would be safe there until Amanda was convicted and the fuss died down. Then he could dig them back up."

Penelope stared at the plastic bags. The silence dragged on painfully. "So, you pretended to be my friend just to hide the stolen jewelry at my house?"

Kaylee wished Penelope sounded angry, but she only seemed hurt.

Andrew remained slumped over in his chair, silent. His bloodshot eyes were sunken in his wrinkled face. He finally met Penelope's gaze. "I know it won't help, but I *am* sorry. I truly enjoy your company." He glanced at Kaylee. "I had supplied Ronnie with the right combination to the safe before I came here to work and before I met Amanda and Madison. I hated it that Amanda was arrested for what we did, but by then it was too late."

For a full minute, nothing was said.

Penelope started to scoop the dirt back into her pot.

"Don't replant your fern with that soil," Kaylee said. "It's too devoid of nutrients. It will cause your plant to weaken and discolor and eventually kill it."

"What? Why?"

"I wondered why we ran short on the special mix I made for Madison's carnivorous plants. Insect-eating plants require a half-peat moss and half-sand mixture. It's very nutrient-poor soil. Your fern needs regular potting soil, which is much different and includes a lot of organic matter, like manure and compost mulch, because the ferns rely on nitrogen."

"The soil you mixed for Madison would kill my fern?" Penelope asked.

"Exactly, although I doubt Andrew realized that. After I read the letter in the well and wondered where the other jewelry was hidden, I recalled Sylvia's annoyance that Andrew had gone to your cottage when you weren't there and repotted plants on your porch, saying they were root-bound. Then my training as a forensic botanist kicked in."

Penelope frowned, bewilderment written on her face. "I don't understand."

"On the way back here today, I swung by your cottage. One look at the wrong soil, and I knew Andrew hadn't repotted your ferns to help you. He'd been in a hurry and grabbed what was at hand here in the shop, which just happened to be Madison's carnivorous soil mixture."

Penelope stared at Andrew, and her face mirrored confusion warring with hurt.

"I'm sorry, Penny. I was supposed to hide the jewelry until Ronnie was set to leave. I pawned that one ring to buy his overseas ticket." Andrew gulped. "And he hid one necklace in Amanda's house to get the sheriff to focus there. I'm ashamed to say that it worked."

Jessica waved her phone in the air. "Should I call the police now?"

Kaylee nodded, then studied Ronald. "You hid the gold pocket watch in the well after I noticed it and commented on it. And you claimed it had been given to you by your grandfather."

Kaylee gazed around the group, noting each individual's reaction: livid Ronald, disconsolate Penelope, guilt-ridden Andrew, exhilarated Jessica, and puzzled Amanda.

Penelope sidled up next to Kaylee and whispered, "Did Andrew really commit a crime? He didn't break into the safe. He only passed along possible combinations, right?"

Kaylee kept her voice gentle. "Possession of stolen goods is a crime, and he hid the jewelry in order to keep it." She put an arm around Penelope's shoulders. "I don't know what will happen, but I do know that Andrew isn't innocent. On the other hand, I'm confident the statute of limitations has run out on the Chicago robbery he participated in."

Jessica hung up her phone. "Sheriff Maddox is on his way."

Bear ran to the door and sat down as if he planned to greet the sheriff as soon as he arrived.

Kaylee hugged Amanda and offered up a huge prayer of gratitude. While Kaylee truly sympathized with Penelope's feelings of betrayal, her overriding sentiment was one of relief for Amanda. The charges would have to be dropped now.

It was all over.

22

The end of the fall festival weekend found Kaylee exhausted. The weekend had been a financial success, but the festival was overshadowed for her by two things: the arrest of Ronald and Andrew Goldfield for the robbery of The Velvet Box and the exoneration of Amanda Denman.

Her friend's release had come with an apology from Sheriff Maddox on the steps of the sheriff's department in Eastsound.

Reese had shown up for the event with a newspaper reporter and a photographer in tow that he'd dragged away from the barbershop quartet concert in the park. "Front and center," he instructed. "You're going to make sure everyone knows Amanda is innocent."

Kaylee grinned at Madison, and they shifted to give the newspeople access to Amanda.

"Thank you." Kaylee had been so grateful to Reese that she could have hugged him right there in front of everyone.

Reese ducked his head. "Amanda's arrest was splashed across the front page of the paper, so her vindication deserves the same publicity."

"I couldn't agree more."

Sunday evening Kaylee folded the newspaper, yawned, and curled up by the fire with one of her grandpa's mysteries. She'd already decided to take Monday off after working nonstop all weekend. She had only one errand to run, and it would be a happy one.

Later when she was standing in front of the open refrigerator trying to decide what to fix for supper, tires crunched on the gravel drive.

Bear streaked through the kitchen, barking excitedly.

Peering out the back porch, Kaylee grinned as Amanda and Madison pulled in. Amanda reached into the back seat and emerged with a huge wicker picnic basket.

Kaylee opened the back door, and Bear raced over to Madison. She knelt and hugged his wriggling body, then picked him up and followed Amanda inside.

"What do you have there?" Kaylee asked, grinning.

Amanda set her basket down. "You haven't eaten yet, have you?"

"No, I was trying to magically conjure up something from the pathetic odds and ends in my refrigerator."

"Good. Can we sit by the fire in the living room?" Madison asked. "We brought a picnic blanket and everything."

Soon the wicker basket was open on the living room floor, and Kaylee leaned back on her hands before the fire. Amanda unpacked the food, and Madison handed out plates, glasses, and silverware.

"I got a variety of things to nibble on." Amanda set out smoked salmon, cheddar cheese, pickles, whole grain crackers and goat cheese, fall pears, and fresh cherries.

Bear's tail whipped back and forth, but it was the only sign that he wanted to sample the goodies.

Kaylee brought Bear's food dish in by the fire so he could be sociable. "Good boy," she whispered.

"Don't worry." Madison took his face in her hands. "I'll share a few bits."

"I hardly know where to start." Kaylee popped a fresh cherry into her mouth. "I have to try everything."

"And later, for dessert"—Madison beat a drumroll on a pillow—"we have peach croissants and dark chocolate."

"A feast fit for a king," Kaylee agreed. "And a great way to celebrate your mom's wonderful news."

"I can't believe it's all over." Amanda spread a red-and-white checked napkin on her lap. "Did you ever suspect Andrew? Or was it a big shock to you too when you found out he was involved?"

Kaylee paused with food halfway to her lips. "I never suspected him at all."

"Me either," Madison said softly. "I always trusted Andrew. I even discussed Mom's case with him once. I guess his attention was just to pump me for information."

"I think you're wrong," Kaylee protested. "Andrew had already given Ronald the combination to the safe before he met you. I truly believe he enjoyed getting to know you. You and Penelope both. I think he was so caught up in being blackmailed by Ronald that he didn't know how to stop."

Amanda frowned. "There's one thing I can't figure out."

"What's that?"

"How did Ronald and Andrew know the location of that old well?"

Kaylee spread goat cheese on her crackers. "I wondered about that too. It turns out Reese told Andrew."

"Reese?" Amanda deposited a spoonful of cherries onto her plate. "How did that happen?"

"Andrew accidentally shut me in the dark closet at the shop one day. The door was stuck, and I panicked a bit when I couldn't get out. Reese checked on the sticky doors for me. Then after I got trapped in the shed and needed Reese to fix some boards I broke off, I told him why it freaked me out so much, how I'd been trapped in the well as a child." She reached for another cracker. "Apparently when Andrew asked him why small, dark places scared me so much, Reese told him about the well at the farm."

Madison twisted her hair around her finger. "I think that Ronald guy is the real criminal. Andrew didn't want to be part of those robberies. He could never hurt someone like when Chloe got hurt."

"Let's be fair," Amanda cautioned. "We talked to Chloe's mom at the medical center this afternoon, and Chloe said no one hit her. She said a car drove very close, and she *thought* it would hit her. It scared her, and she jumped backward and tripped. That's how she hit her head on a rock."

"So how's Chloe doing?" Kaylee asked.

"She has a concussion," Madison said, helping herself to more cheese and pickles. "I took a teddy bear over yesterday and left it at the front desk. Today the nurses let me see her for ten minutes."

"What did Chloe want to tell you?" Kaylee asked, accepting a peach croissant and a square of dark chocolate from Amanda.

"She overheard Ronald talking to Andrew about the missing jewelry under the bleachers. They stopped talking when they saw her. She said Andrew told her some lame story to explain away what she'd heard, but she didn't buy it."

"I'm just glad that Chloe had nothing to do with the robberies." Amanda yawned twice. "I guess it's time to think about going. I'll clean up this mess first. Picnic or not, we don't want your living room overrun with ants."

Kaylee patted her full stomach and sighed contentedly. "What now? Do you want your old job back since you've been proven innocent?"

"I couldn't go back to that job, even if I wanted to." Amanda folded up the blanket, stepped out on the porch, and shook out the crumbs. Back inside, she said, "Mr. LeMasters told me that the jewelry store really is being sold but not because of financial trouble. Mr. Liddon is taking early retirement, and he and his wife plan to travel."

"Speaking of Mr. Liddon," Kaylee said, "I'm still wondering why he thanked Thomas for his help and gave him a bonus in his paycheck."

"I know the answer to that mystery," Amanda announced. "I heard that Thomas did some work around the jewelry store to get it ready to go on the market."

Kaylee wrapped her arms around her bent knees. "So, what will you do now?"

"I'm not sure," Amanda admitted with a sigh.

"I want to move back to Oregon," Madison piped up. "Even with Mom being found innocent, the kids at school will always remember and act funny around me after this."

Kaylee wanted to argue the point, but she suspected Madison was right, at least for a while.

Madison turned pleading eyes on her mother. "We could move back home during Thanksgiving break if Mom would just say yes. I want to forget this terrible time."

Kaylee stood, then grabbed the poker and stirred the fire. "I can understand that, but you both would truly be missed."

Amanda stacked the used plates. "I honestly love it here, but Orcas Island is an expensive place for this single-income family to live. I could never afford to buy us even a small house here."

"Then let's move back home," Madison urged.

Amanda lifted her shoulders and then let them drop. "I would like to, honey, but moving and making a fresh start somewhere less expensive would still cost money."

"I can help with that," Kaylee said.

"You're so kind," Amanda said, "but I won't take a loan from you."

"I'm not suggesting a loan." Kaylee could barely contain her excitement. "Joseph Liddon offered a reward for the recovery of the store's stolen jewelry. Remember?"

"Yes, but *you* caught the thieves."

"I know, but you and Madison suffered the most by the false accusation. So I accepted the reward money, but I had Joseph make out the check to you." She retrieved the check from her purse and handed it to Amanda. "Here."

Amanda and Madison stared openmouthed at the amount.

Madison squealed, setting off Bear's barking, and together they danced around the living room.

Amanda covered her mouth with a hand that trembled. "I can't believe this."

"I will miss you both so much," Kaylee said, "but I want you to be happy. This should be enough to tide you over while you get resettled. You just have to promise me that you'll come back to visit."

They talked for a while longer, but soon it was time to go. Amanda tapped Madison on the knee. "You've still got school tomorrow, young lady."

"Do I have to go, now that we're moving back home?"

"We aren't moving tomorrow," Amanda reminded her. "It will be a few weeks before I can get all our ducks in a row."

"Oh. Okay." Madison gave Kaylee an enormous hug, then did another dance around the room with a barking Bear in her arms.

Kaylee was reading her book, cozy before the fire, when the phone rang. She was reluctant to answer it. After such a high-intensity whirlwind of a weekend, she wanted to hang on to her drowsy state and sink into a well-deserved night of deep sleep.

She sighed and rose to get her phone. But when she saw it was Mary, she smiled and quickly picked up.

"How did the fall festival weekend go?" Mary asked without preamble.

"It was fabulous—a huge moneymaker for the Island Grove charity. Sandra beamed and swelled up like a peacock when the Petals presented her with a large check."

"I'm sorry I wasn't there to help you hold down the fort. Now, be honest. Has it all just been too boring without me?"

Kaylee burst out laughing. Then she settled into her chair with Bear curled in her lap. "Mary, have I got a tale for you."

YOUR FEEDBACK MEANS A LOT TO US!

Up to this point, we've been doing all the writing. Now it's *your* turn!

Tell us what you think about this book, the characters, the bad guy, or anything else you'd like to share with us about this series. We can't wait to hear from *you*!

Log on to give us your feedback at:

https://www.surveymonkey.com/r/FlowerShopMysteries

Annie's FICTION